MARRIED TO DA STREETS

A NOVEL BY

SILK WHITE

GOOD2GOPUBLISHING

Published by:
GOOD2GOPUBLISHING
7311 W. Glass Lane
Laveen, AZ 85339
www.good2gopublishing.com
facebook/silkwhite
twitter@silkwhite
silkwhite212@yahoo.com
Ravon@good2gopublishing.com

ThirdLane Marketing: Brian James
Brian@good2gopublishing.com

ISBN: 978-1-4243-3079-9

Typeset by Rukyyah

DEDICATIONS

This book is dedicated to all the people in every hood who gotta get it how they live and know about the struggle.

To all my people locked behind the wall keep ya head up. It gets greater later. You smell me?

CHAPTER ONE

Rico stepped out his Mom's crib and couldn't wait to get downstairs. His mother was high and was talking him to death! "Damn she talks too fuckin much when she gets high" Rico said to himself as he went and took a seat on the bench outside. Rico hated living in the projects and he especially hated living with his mother. As soon as he got enough money to leave, that's what he was going to do. "Damn I gotta get some fucking paper". Rico said to himself with his head down in deep thought. He looked up, and saw Trina one of his close friends that he had grew up with heading in his direction.

"What you doing sitting out here by yourself" Trina asked, interrupting Ricos thought helping herself to a seat on the bench next to him. Trina was dark skin with hair that came down to her shoulders, she had a fat ass and a perfect set of tits. Her and Rico grew up together, so he looked at her like the sister he never had.

"Just chillin Ma, you know same shit different day" Rico replied.

"I hear dat shit" Trina said as said sitting up on top of the bench.

"Where Jason"? Rico asked.

"You know J Murder is at da gym doing his boxing thang, he has what it takes to make it" Trina said looking at her watch.

"Yo what you lookin at ya watch for?" Rico asked bodily.

"Cuz nigga I got a date tonight" Trina responded with a smile. At first she didn't want to tell Rico, because she knew how protective him, and J-Murder was when it came to her, ut she knew if she didn't tell him some how the word would still get.

"Wit Who?"

"Some guy I met yesterday while I was downtown" Trina shot back. "Now if you'll excuse me, I gotta go get ready" Trina said playfully. Rico didn't really trust other guys around Trina, but he knew even if he told her not to go, she would of still went anyway, so he didnt even bother wasting his breath.

"Aight be careful and don't be letting that nigga feel ya butt neither" He called out.

"Rico you know I don't even get down like that" she said slightly offended.

"Nah, I'm just fuckin wit you, yo have a good time"

"You know I am" Trina winked as she broke out.

Rico sat on the bench eating sun flower seeds until it got dark. He was sitting there drinking his quarter water when he saw Jason walking towards his building.

"A yo J Murder, what's good nigga"? Rico yelled throwing his hands up in the air.

"What's good my dude"? J Murder said as he gave Rico a pound. "What da fuck you doin sittin out here by yourself"?

"My mom's high again and talking a nigga ear off, I rather sit outside by myself than inside listening to her talk shit all day feel me?"

"I hear dat shit" J Murder said taking a seat next to Rico. He knew how Rico's mother got when she got high so he could definately feel his best friend's pain. J-Murder was built like Mike Tyson, but he had the strength and power of Mike Tyson with the swiftness of Roy Jones. He was known in the hood for knocking niggas out. J-Murder had been boxing since he was 11 years old, his dream was to win the Heavyweight Title one day. With the skills he had his dreams were definatel within his reach...all he had to do was remain focused.

"Yo come wit me to the Chinese restaurant real quick" J-Murder said as the two walked to the Chinese restaurant. As Rico and J-Murder headed to the Chinese Resturant they saw Smoke chilling on a bench with a few hoes from the projects. Now

Smoke had the whole projects on smash with the crack. He was a hood legend and a ghetto superstar. Smoke was not the wild type but if you fucked with his money it would definitely be hell to pay. Everybody respected and liked Smoke. He was a drug dealer but with the money he made, he'd tried to make the projects a better place for the kids. Everyone called him Smoke cuz he was black as train smoke! Plus he smoked weed all day, every day so the name just kind of stuck with him.

"What's poppin Smoke"? Rico said giving him a pound.

"If I call it, I might spoil it" Smoke answered smiling flashing a mouth full of gold teeth.

"So what's up? When you gonna put me on so I can start making some money"? Rico asked.

"Put you on?" Smoke echoed looking at the youngster like he was crazy. "You got your whole future ahead of you, you don't need to be out here in these streets. You need to be in college getting ya education". Smoke said kickin some knowledge.

"Man fuck college! What the fuck can a book teach me that I don't already know? I'm hungry right now and I need to get dis paper!" Rico said as if he was saying something big.

"So you think it's just that simple huh? U think you can just sell crack and make money right?" Smoke asked.

"Basically" Rico said nonchalantly.

"That's where you wrong lil nigga, you got to be a hustling, heartless muthafucka to make it out here on these streets. If you not a real hustler you won't last very long in this business, and to be honest I just don't see the hustle in you" Smoke said as his cell phone rang. "Yo I gotta go take care of some business but I'll talk to you later Rico" Smoke said as he walked off talking on his phone.

When Rico and J Murder made it inside the Chinese restaurant both men ordered chicken wings and pork fried rice. "You see that's what I'm talking bout" J-Murder said as he sipped his Snapple. "Mufuckas ain't gonna give us shit, we got to go out there and take it! Like Lil Kim said "first you get the money, then you get the power, then mufuckas will respect you" I don't know about you but mufuckas is gonna start to respect my gangsta B. Is you wit me or what?"

"You mufuckin right I'm wit you" Rico answered. "As a matter of fact I got a little plan on how we can get some paper Is you in?"

J-Murder looked at Rico and smiled. "Let's do this my nigga"

"Aight so tomorrow when you come home from the gym, come stop by my crib, either we gonna ball hard or fall hard," Rico said as the two men grabbed their food and headed home.

When Rico stepped in his crib, his mother Janet was playing cards with her get high partner

Pam. "Where have you been all day?" Janet asked, with her two eyes looking like peppermint balls.

"What da fuck does it matter where I have been all day"? Rico shot back.

"You better watch your got damn mouth boy, I am still your mother and you will respect me"

Rico ignored his mothers comment as he walked in his room and slammed the door behind him. Rico threw his food on the dresser and went straight to his radio and threw on his theme song, "Ballin" by Jim Jones. He then sat down and enjoyed his food. he spent most of his time either out in the streets, or his just so he didnt have to hear his mother huffing, and complaining about petty shit.

The next day Rico was sitting in his room chilling with Trina waiting for J Murder to come home from the gym. They both had a nervous look on their faces.

"So what's with ya big plan"? Trina asked.

"It's simple, you know Teddy right?"

"The Jamaican dat sells weed?" she asked.

"Yeah we gonna rob that nigga tonight!"

"Rob him wit what"? Trina asked.

"Wit these" Rico said pulling out two B.B. guns. He knew this was a big risk he was taking, but it was either this, or be broke, and being broke was something he couldn't do anymore.

"Ain't thoses B.B. guns"? Trina asked examining one of the toy guns.

"Yeah" Rico smiled.

"So what happens if you got to shot him?" Trina said placing the B.B. Gun back on the dresser.

"Don't worry about all that just let me and J handle this" Rico told her.

"All I know is ya'll better get that money" Trina said playfully. As Rico and Trina continued to talk, Rico heard a knock at the door. When he looked through the peep hole he saw that it was J Murder.

"What's good, you ready to go handle dis"? Rico asked giving J-Murder a pound.

"Let's go get dis money" J-Murder answered quickly. Rico handed J Murder a B.B. gun and a ski mask as the two headed out. the door. As Rico and J Murder headed to Teddy's crib they ran into Smoke coming out of Teddy's building.

"What's good boys?" He greeted the two young gansters.

"Chillin Smoke, tryin to get dis money" Rico said proudly.

"I'm gonna give ya'll niggas a little advice" Smoke said. "Make sure ya'll niggas know what ya'll getting into before ya'll just jump into shit, cuz its real out here in these streets you gotta be ready for anything" He said lifting up his shirt and showing Rico and J-Murder the butt of his Desert Eagle. "But yo I gotta go check up on some shit B, I'll holla at ya'll niggas later ya'll hold it down out here" Smoke said as he went on about his business.

When Rico and J-Murder finally made it to Teddy's door both men threw on their ski mask and pulled out their B.B guns. J-Murder was just about to kick Teddy's door in when he saw some hood rat bitch get off the elevator on Teddy's floor.

"Move bitch and I'll blow ya fuckin brains out!" J-Murder said as he aimed the B.B gun at her head. Rico then grabbed a hand full of the hood rat's weave.

"Get over here bitch, knock on the fuckin door and tell Teddy you need some weed or I'mma kill you" Rico growled as he pressed the B.B. gun in the back of the hood rats head.

"Okay, okay just don't hurt me" The girl said as she knocked on the door.

"Who is it?" Teddy screamed from behind the door.

"It's me Sandy" The hood rat said in a friendly tone. When J-Murder saw the door crack he pushed his way inside and bust Teddy in the head with the toast (gun), sending Teddy crashing to the floor.

"Yo what da Bumbaclot" Teddy yelled as he hit the floor. Rico then threw the hood rat bitch on the floor next to Teddy.

"Okay mufucka, I'm only gonna ask you once, where's da shit?"

"Me have no clue what you talk bout" Teddy replied

WHACK! J-Murder cracked him with the toast again. "Open ya mouth mufucka!"

"Okay, okay mon" Teddy said raising his hand not wanting to get hit again. "I got 15 pounds of Skunk in the bathroom, and I got $10,000 dollars in the bedroom under the mattress, just don't kill me" he said holding his bloody forehead. Rico held Teddy and the hood rat bitch at gun point, while J-Murder went and searched the bathroom and the bedroom. When J Murder got in the bathroom he looked under the sink and found two duffle bags full of weed, he threw both duffle bags around his neck and headed to the bedroom. He violently threw the mattress off the bed and found $10,000 cash along with a .45 hand gun. He quickly threw the money in one of the duffle bags and put the heat in his waistband, and headed back to the living room.

"What's up everything straight"? Rico asked with a desperate look in his eyes.

"Yeah everything good!" J-Murder smiled.

"Aight hold me down while I tape these mufuckas up" Rico said.

After Rico taped Teddy and the hood rat up him and J-Murder quickly exited Teddy's crib. By the time they reached the building Trina was right their waiting for them.

"So what's up everything went alright?" Trina asked as they got on the elevator.

"Yo we gonna talk when we get upstairs, you never know who's listening" Rico stated with sweat trickling down the side od his face. When they made it to J-Murder's room he dumped everything on his bed. Rico then took the $10,000 kept $4,000 for himself, gave J $4,000 and gave Trina $2,000.

"Yo, this right here is just the beginning B." Rico said counting his money. Inside he felt good, not because he had some money now, but because if he knew if he ever had to do it again he could.

"So how ya'll gonna sell that weed?" Trina asked sniffing one of the big bags of weed.

"Yo first thang tomorrow I'm gonna holla at dat nigga Goggles. I'm gonna have dat nigga move it all for us" Rico said.

"And what makes you think he's just gonna sell 15 pounds of weed for us when he got his own shit? J-Murder asked.

"Cuz I'm gonna make him an offer he can't refuse" Rico said smiling.

"Oh shit! I almost forgot to show you what else we got from Teddy" J-Murder said pulling out the .45

"That's what's up, let me see that hammer (gun), yo we gotta share this shit" Rico said looking like a psycho with the gun in his hand. "Let me hold this shit down in the daytime and you can hold it down at night when you get home from the gym" -

"Sounds good to me" J-Murder said. "But yo I gotta get some sleep right now B so I'm gonna holla at ya'll tomorrow"

"Aight my nigga I'm gonna go take this shit to Trina's crib, cause knowing my luck, my Mom's might fuck around find it and sell it before I can" Rico said playfully. While Rico walked Trina to her crib he felt tougher and braver carrying the heat (gun). When they made it to Trina's crib Rico made sure she was straight, kissed her on the cheek and broke out.

Rico stuck his key in the door and entered his crib. When he stepped inside he saw Janet sitting on the couch with some big diesel nigga.

"What's up lil nigga"? The diesel nigga said to Rico.

"Lil nigga?" Rico repeated. "Who the fuck is you talking to like that?" Rico snarled taking a step closer in the mans direction.

"Watch ya mouth" Janet cut in. "This is your uncle Kenny. He just came home from doing 10 years in Elmira, you don't remember him?"

"Yeah I remember him" Rico lied. "What's up Kenny?"

"You tell me Rico the last time I saw you, you was like 8 years old" Kenny grinned.

"Yeah I know, but yo I gotta go take care of something, so I'm gonna have to holla at you tomorrow B." Rico said as he headed for his room.

"Rico" Janet shouted. "Your uncle is going to be staying wit us until he finds his own place, are you okay with that?"

"I don't care" Rico responded as he slammed his door. It was some thing funny about his uncle but he couldn't put his finger on it. Something about him just screamed trouble.

The next day Rico went to the payphone and called Goggles. the phone rung four times before someone picked up. "Hello?"

"Yo what's up can I speak to Goggles?" Rico asked.

"Yeah this Goggles who this?"

"Rico"

"What's up you need some Chronic?" Goggles asked wondering why Rico was calling him.

"Nah I need to holla at you about something, meet me in front of my building in 5 minutes"

"Yo gimme like 10 minutes" Goggles said ending the phone call. Rico was sitting in front of his building sippin on his Orange juice when Goggles walked up.

"What's on your mind my nigga?" Goggles asked giving Rico a pound.

"Just wanted to talk a little business with you" Rico told him. Now Goggles was the type of nigga who knew how to get money. He had all the customers but he never had enough product to really blow up and most of the time when somebody wanted some weight he couldn't cover the order.

"Yo listen B, I got 15 pounds of Skunk. I'll front you all 15 but I want $1500 for each one" Rico offered him.

"Where the fuck you get 15 pounds from?" Goggles asked.

"Stop asking so many questions" Rico said as he shot goggles a cold stare before he continued. "Nigga you want the weed are not?"

"Yeah, yeah I'll take it off your hands, $1500 a joint right?"

"That's what I said, sell it how you see fit just have my paper, when it's time to get paid I don't want to have to come looking for you" Rico warned.

"Come on Baby I don't even get down like dat B. You already know Rico I'm about my business" Goggles said like he was trying to convince himdelf rather then Rico.

"Aight B. I'ma bring that 15 to ya crib in 30 minutes aight?" Rico said as he gave Goggles a pound and headed to Trina's crib.

CHAPTER TWO

Smoke pulled up in front of a building in Hunts Point in the Bronx in his CLK 430 Benz. Him and his main man Dred hopped out and headed upstairs to handle some business. Dred was Smoke's main man. He had Dredlocks and the ladies said he looked like Lil Wayne. He also had a mouth full of gold, his money was long but not as long as Smoke's. Him and Smoke had been partners since elementary school, not only partners but best friends. When Smoke and Dred reached the apartment they were looking for they quickly drew their weapons. On the count of three Dred kicked in the door. When Smoke and Dred entered the living room they saw some fat man eating some woman's pussy.

"Get ya fat ass up Victor" Smoke yelled as he aimed his Desert Eagle at Victor's head.

"Oh shit....chill Smoke put dat fuckin gun down" Victor said wiping his mouth embarrassed that he'd just gotten caught performing oral sex on his lady friend.

"Where the fuck is my money, it's been a month already" Smoke huffed.

"Wait Smoke, I don't have ya money but I called my cousin Hollywood he lives out in L.A., and he said he sending one of his men to bring me the money next week" Victor explained.

"Mufucka you was suppose to have my money two weeks ago," Smoke growled in an angry tone. As Smoke was screaming on Victor, the young lady who was getting her pussy ate hopped up.

"Excuse me, but do you think I could put my clothes on and leave? Cuz this has nothing to do wit me".

Dred's eyes were glued on the young woman's fat ass and firm breast. "Yo bitch nobody leaves unless I tell them to" Dred said to the young woman. The young woman noticed how Dred was looking at her so she came up with a plan to try and save her life.

"Excuse me" She said politely.

"What is it bitch?" Dred said disrespectfully.

"Is there anything I can do to help ya'll out?, and I do mean anything"

Dred looked at the young woman's fat ass and said, "as a matter of fact, it is something that you can do" He said as he pulled his dick out. "Come over here and let me get some head fakes (oral sex)". The young woman walked right up to Dred and threw his dick in her mouth. Dred watched the young woman's mouth slide up and down his dick. She then started deep throating his dick and massaging his balls all at the same time. Dred then pulled out and rolled a condom on his dick, "yo bend over". The young woman bent over and placed her hands on the kitchen table. Dred immediately dove right in and started blowing the young woman's back out.

"So how much you got right now B.?" Smoke asked running out of patience.

"Yo I'm telling you next week my cousin Hollywood is sending one of his..." WHACK!

"Mufucka you think I'm stupid?" Smoke said as he back slapped Victor with the heat (gun). "Yo where you want it at, the head or the chest?"

"Don't do this Smoke, I'll have the money next week!" Victor pleaded.

"Okay have it ya mufuckin way!" BOOM...BOOM. Smoke popped Victor in the head and the chest. "Okay lover boy that's enough" BOOM! Smoke put a bullet in the woman who Dred was piping head.

"Damn nigga you could have at least waited to I bust a nut" Dred said laughing. The two men hopped in the Benz and broke out.

***

A week had passed and everything with Rico and Goggles was going fine. Goggles was doing his thang and had the hood on smash with the Chronic.

"Yo I'mma holla at you in a minute, I gotta go get something to eat" Rico said as he walked to the corner to catch a cab. "Yo take me to Popeye's on Fordham Road" Rico said as he hopped in the Lincoln. When Rico stepped in the restaurant the lines were OD long. After about 15 minutes of waiting it was finally his turn to order.

"Hi welcome to Popeye's, can I take ya order?" The cashier asked.

When Rico looked up he couldn't believe his eyes. He was standing face to face with the prettiest girl he had ever seen. "Yeah let me get two spicy breast, some fries, a biscuit, a iced tea and I'll take your number along with that" he said flashing a smile.

The cashier smiled and went to go get Rico's food. She came back a minute later. "I'm sorry but your gonna have to wait 5 minutes for the fries"

"It's all good" Rico said looking at the cashier's name tag that read Tiffany. "So Tiffany, what's a pretty girl like ya self doing working at Popeye's?"

"I gotta take care of myself, ain't nobody giving me no handouts and I damn sure ain't looking for none" She told him.

"I hear that Ma, but what's up? You think I could get ya number and call you sometime? Go out, get something to eat or something like that?" Rico asked.

"No, I'm sorry I don't even know you and I don't give my number to strangers" Tiffany said as she went to get Rico's food. "Okay Sir you have a nice day"

Rico pulled out a pen and wrote down his number and handed it to Tiffany. "You have a nice day dap Ma, make sure I hear from you aight".

"I'll think about it" Tiffany said with a smile. Rico then caught a cab back to the hood.

Later on that night Rico, J-Murder, and Trina were chilling on the bench with a couple of friends just shooting the breeze. Rico sat back and watched how Smoke's workers were getting money. He noticed how sloppy they were and how easily they were distracted.

"How Smoke put these dumb mufuckas on and not me" Rico thought to himself. His thoughts were interrupted when Smoke walked up on him.

"What's good my nigga"? Smoke asked giving Rico a pound.

"Ain't nothing poppin out here" Rico responded.

"So I hear you and Goggles is shutting shit down out here wit the trees (weed)"

"Yeah, I thought about what you said, about being a real hustler to make it out here and now I'm focused on getting this paper"

"You see that's what I'm talking about, get ya mind right and maybe me and you could do some business, hold on" Smoke said as he answered his phone. As Smoke answered his cell phone Rico noticed an unfamiliar face standing by the flag pole. Something was funny about the man because it was the middle of the summer but the man was wearing a hoodie.

"Something is definitely wrong with this picture" Rico thought to himself. Smoke hung up his phone and gave Rico a pound. "Yo I gotta go handle some shit real quick, I'll catch up wit you later".

As Smoke headed to the next building Rico noticed that the man wearing the hoodie begin to follow Smoke. "Yo J-Murder let me get that ratchet (gun)"

"Why, what's up?"

"I gotta go take care of something" Rico said as he took the ratchet and followed the man wearing the hoodie. When Smoke made it inside the building he pressed the call button for the elevator, three minutes later the elevator had finally arrived. As Smoke entered the elevator he heard somebody behind him. When he turned around he was face to face with a .45 The man wearing the hoodie pushed Smoke to the back of the elevator and pressed the button to the top floor. The hoodie man then snatched Smoke's Desert Eagle from his waist band and smacked him across the face with it.

"Hollywood told me to deliver a message to you, you fuck wit his people you die simple as that"

"Yo I don't know what you talking about" Smoke said with a mouth full of blood.

"Mufucka you know exactly what I'm talking about cuz" The hooded man said in L.A. accent. "You killed Hollywood's cousin Victor. Now you gotta pay" The hoodied man said as they reached the top floor.

When Rico made it to the building he had just missed the elevator that Smoke and the hoodied man got on. Rico pressed the button for the other elevator as he counted how many floors Smoke's elevator went up. The elevator finally arrived and Rico hopped on and pressed the top floor. When Rico reached the top floor he pulled out the .45 and headed up to the roof.

Smoke stood on the roof scared to death. He just knew he was gonna die.

"Listen up you mark ass trick, you got two choices, you can either jump off the roof or take a couple of bullets, the choice is yours" said the hoodied man. "What's it gonna be?"

"Check this out" Smoke said pleading for his life. "Yo I'll give you whatever you want just don't kill me"

"Stop bitchin and man up" the hoodied man snarled. "Now I'm gonna count to three and if you ain't made a choice yet I'm gonna shoot you and throw you off the roof! "1, 2, before the count of 3 Rico came charging through the door gun already in hand. BOOM....BOOM... BOOM. Rico shot the hoodied man three times in the back sending crashing into the pebbles. When Smoke saw Rico pop the hoodied man, he wanted to give Rico a hug. Instead he ran and grabbed his Desert Eagle from off the ground and grabbed the hoodied man.

"Turn around you bitch ass nigga" Smoke said turning him over. "Listen give me Hollywood's address and I swear I won't kill you"

"Fuck you!" The hoodied man said as he started laughing hysterically as blood leaked from the corners of his mouth. Smoke then stuck his Desert Eagle in the man's mouth and pulled the trigger.

"Come on let's throw this mufucka off the roof" Rico said as he stuck his gun back in his waist band.

"Nah, be easy we can't do that" said Smoke.

"Why not?"

"Cuz if you throw this nigga off the roof the hood is gonna be flooded wit cops and once they start investigating thats gonna be the end of getting money in the projects. Now if he didn't have so many bullet holes in his ass then maybe we could throw him off the roof and make it look like a suicide. As Rico and Smoke finished talking they heard the staircase door open. Both men immediately drew their weapons and was shocked to see J-Murder standing there holding a knife.

"Damn nigga I almost popped you" Rico said putting his burner (gun) back in his waist band. "You can't be running up on nihave like that"

"What the fuck you expect me to do"? J-Murder said hooking his knife back on his belt. "I saw you and Smoke go in the building, then minutes later I hear gunshots so I came to make sure my nigga was aight"

"So what was you gonna do with the knife?"Smoke laughed.

"I don't know I was gonna do something" J-Murder said giving Smoke a pound.

"I gotta give it to ya'll niggaz, ya'll got heart but let's talk about this later" Smoke said. "Now we gotta get this cleaned up" he said as he called up Dred.

"Yeah, what's up?"

"I need you to holla at the clean up crew for me" Smoke said speaking in codes over the phone.

"Why, what happen?"

"I'll explain later, tell them building five on Pebbles Beach (the roof) and tell them to be quick One" Smoke hung up his phone and the three men left the scene of the crime.

CHAPTER THREE

Two days later Rico was chilling in the projects with Goggles and Trina when his cell phone rung. He looked at the caller ID but couldn't recognize the number. "Yo who this" he answered.

"Hi, can I speak to Rico?" A female voice asked politely.

"Yecal this Rico who This?"

"Tiffany the girl from Popeye's"

"What's good Ma?"

"Nothing I was just chilling and I came across your number, and decided to give you a ring" Tiffany said.

"That's what's up, so when you gonna come through and check the kid?" Rico asked smoothly. inside he was just happy that she had called him.

"When you tryin to see me?" she asked.

"Whenever you available"

"What you doing tonight?"

"I ain't doing shit tonight Ma, why you gonna come through and keep me company?" Rico said flicking his wrist so he could look at his watch.

"I think I can do dat, what time you want me to come through?"

"Come through around 9:00pm."

"Aight Rico I'll see you at 9:00" she said ending the call.

When Rico hung up his phone he saw Dred coming his way. "What's poppin Dred?" Rico said giving him a pound.

"I'm chilling Smoke sent me over here to get you" Dred said.

"For what?" Rico asked curiously.

"He didn't say, he Just said he needed to holla at you"

"Yo Trina, I'll be right back" he said as him, and Dred disappeared into the next building. When Rico and Dred made it to one of the stash cribs Smoke came out the back with a smile on his face. "Make yourself at home" Smoke said as he sat down.

"So what's poppin" Rico asked as he got comfortable.

"Well it's like this, you saved my life the other day and I wanted to repay you" Smoke said tossing Rico a book bag. Rico caught the book bag, looked inside and saw money neatly stacked in rubber bands. "What's this?"

"It's money, that's $10,000 in there" Smoke said pointing to the book bag.

"I'm sorry Smoke but I can't accept your money" Rico said tossing the book bag back to Smoke.

"Why not?"

"Cause I don't want ya money, if you really wanna repay me then you would put me on" Rico suggested.

"I don't know" Smoke said."If you fuck up one time it's a wrap"

"Say no more" Rico said with a big smile.

"Here's a little free advice, never turn down free money" Smoke said tossing the book bag to Rico. "I got something else for you too" Smoke said as he went to the back room. When he returned he handed him two brand new 9mm's. "Since you running shit now I know you gonna need some heat"

"Good lookin Smoke you got my word I ain't gonna let you down B., but if I'm gonna be running thangs then I'm gonna have to make some changes"

"Listen Rico you run it how you see fit. As long as I get my money on time then I'm good, but don't forget you have to be fare cause my workers work hard so make sure you pay them good"

"Yeah, no doubt everybody gonna eat". As Rico was getting ready to bounce he threw the two 9mm's in his book bag.

"Hold up before you leave do you still have that four fifth that you used the other night?" Smoke asked.

"Yeah I still got it" Rico said lifting up his shirt revealing the butt of the four fifth.

"Why don't you let me have dat so I could get rid of it"

"No disrespect Smoke but I think I should get rid of it myself, you know better safe then sorry" Rico said

"I can respect that" Smoke said giving Rico a pound."

"Oh yeah Smoke I don't want to be asking for too much but do you think I could get an extra ratchet?"

"Sure no problem kid"

"I'll take a .380 if you have one." Rico requested. Minutes later Dred came out the back room carrying a chrome 9mm. "Ain't no .380's back there"

"Aight this will do" Rico said as he stuffed the 9mm in his bag. "Tomorrow morning I'mma get shit poppin"Rico said as he gave both Smoke and Dred both pounds and exited the stash crib feeling like he had just hit the lotto.

"So what's up Smoke? You think we did the right thang by putting him on?" Dred asked while sipping some apple juice. He didnt trust Rico, and felt he was too young to be holding down an entire housing project on his own.

"Yeah he might be young but he's smart, he's on point and he has heart, We just gonna see how it plays out. But I'm telling you right now the boy got what it takes" Smoke assured his right hand man.

"I hope you right Smoke" Dred said as he gave Smoke a pound and broke out.

Later on that night Rico stood in front of his building with Trina and J-Murder explaining how he was gonna take over when he was interrupted by his cell phone vibrating. "Yo" he answered.

"Hello I can I speak to Rico?" The voice on the other end asked.

"Yeah this Rico, what's poppin?"

"What's up, this Tiffany we still on for tonight right?"

"Of course Ma"

"Aigh't I'm on my way"

"Aight I'll be in front of the building waiting for you" Rico said ending the call, and continued discussing his plan with J-Murder and Trina. "Yo we gonna have a meeting tomorrow early in the morning so make sure ya'll get some rest B" As Rico was talking he noticed a cab pull up and out stepped Tiffany. Tiffany was light skin wit a fat ass and some big ass tits. She looked a little like Jada Pinkett except her hair came down to her mid back.

"What's up Rico" Tiffany said giving Rico a hug.

"I'm happy you made it Ma looking all good and shit" Rico said smiling. "Yo dis my man J-Murder and dis my girl Trina.

"Hi it's nice to meet the both of you" Tiffany said politely.

"Yeah it's nice to meet you too Ma" J-Murder said as he gave Rico a pound. "Yo I'mma holla at you tomorrow B." J said as he left to give the two some privacy.

"Yo I'mma grab some Dutchess real quick, you want anything from the store?" Rico asked.

Married To Da Streets

"Nah, I'm good" Tiffany said. Rico looked over.

"Yeah let me get an Orange juice" she said.

"Aight I'll be right back" Rico said as he ran across the street to the store.

"Okay let me get dis out the way from the beginning, I see Rico is feeling you and all that , but I'mma tell you like This, Rico is like my older brother so you better make sure you treat him right cause if you don't you gonna have to answer to me", Trina said wit an attitude. "And trust and believe I have no problem cutting a bitch feel me"

"First of all I'm feeling Rico just as much as he is feeling me" Tiffany said making sure she had Trina's full attention. "Second of all I don't care if you his sister or what, you put ya hands on me you better be ready to scrap straight up" Tiffany shot back matching Trina's attitude.

"Hey what you two over here talking about?" Rico asked as he came back from the store.

"Oh nothing just chit chattin...you know girl talk" Trina said as she kissed Rico on the cheek. "Yo I'mma holla at you later, ya'll have a good time" Trina said shooting Tiffany a private look as she left.

When Rico and Tiffany stepped into the crib Janet and Kenny were sitting in the living room playing cards.

"Hey Rico" Janet said when she seen her son come through the door.

"What's up Ma, I want you to meet Tiffany" he said introducing her to his mother.

"Oh how you doing Tiffany?"

"I'm fine Ma'am"

As Rico and Tiffany headed towards Rico's room they were stopped by Kenny. "Oh, so you ain't gonna introduce ya uncle to this lovely lady right here" he said looking Tiffany up and down on his jail shit.

"Yo Tiffany this is my uncle Kenny, Kenny dis is Tiffany" Rico said dryly.

"It's nice to meet you Kenny" Tiffany said politely.

"No Baby the pleasure is all mine" Kenny said as he kissed Tiffany's hand. "Damn boy you got good taste like ya uncle.

"Yeah whatever" Rico said as him and Tiffany headed to his room. Once inside his room Rico apologized for his uncle's behavior. Just the site of Kenny disgusted Rico, he wanted to smack his uncle's head through the wall sometimes.

"Don't worry about it, it's nothing" Tiffany said brushing it off.

"Nah, I can't stand dat nigga he gonna make me fuck around and clap him" Rico said seriously.

"Calm down Rico it's not dat serious" Tiffany said trying to calm him down. Rico and Tiffany got to know each other better as they passed the blunt back and forth, and drunk wine for hours.

"Well Rico it's getting late, I think I should be heading home now" Tiffany suggested.

Rico and Tiffany stepped in the pissy elevator and headed downstairs. After trying for about twenty minutes Rico finally caught Tiffany a cab. "Yo call me and let me know dat you made it home safe"

"Aight I got you" Tiffany said as she kissed Rico on the cheek and hopped in the cab and went home.

CHAPTER FOUR

In the next week Rico made some major changes in the projects, he switched up the whole hustle instead of moving work in front of the buildings, he had Smoke's worker moving work from inside of the buildings just to keep everything low key, on top of that he had lookouts on the roofs and one of Smoke's workers in front of each building directing the fiends. Rico even bought all the workers walkie talkies just to make sure he had a way to communicate with all of his workers. Rico had J-Murder around to watch his back at all times. One of the 9mm that Rico got from Smoke now belong to J-Murder and the other one now belonged to Trina. Rico also hired Wolverine for security. Now Wolverine was a straight animal, he just did not give a fuck! The only thing he cared about was getting paid and busting his gun. Wolverine never left the house without having his two Berettas on him, any problems in the projects Wolverine's job was to solve them. Rico was making a killing the way he set shit up in the projects so he decided to treat himself to something nice. Rico went out and copped himself an iced out bracelet, along with an iced out bezeled Rolex. The streets were talking so Rico gave them something to talk about. Rico and his crew was chilling in front of building 3 when Rico's cell phone stated ringing. Rico looked at his caller

ID and saw that it was Trina. "Yeah what's poppin?"

"Rico where you at?"

"I'm in front of building 3, why wassup" Rico asked.

""I'm wit some clown right now at the movies and he keep talking about all this paper he got....all you gotta do is give me the word"

"Word?" Rico asked. "What he riding on?"

"He's pushing a Navigator wit some 20's on its feet" Trina told him.

"Bring the nigga through make him think you gonna give him some pussy, and I'll take it from there" he said ending the call. "Yo ya'll niggas keep ya eyes open Trina's coming through witH a victim"

Forty five minutes later Rico saw an all black Navigator pull up with the system bumping, seconds later Trina stepped out. She had on some skin tight pants with some high heel Gucci boots and the Gucci skirt to match. She was followed by some tall cat wearing a T Mac jersey. Once Trina and her friend got close to the building they were met by J-Murder.

"Oh shit, what's poppin?" Trina said as he gave J-Murder a pound. In one quick motion he turned and caught Trina's friend with a right hook to the jaw knocking him out cold!

"Get up you bitch ass nigga" J-Murder said as he took the man's keys from his pockets. Once J-Murder peeled off in the Navigator. Wolverine and the rest of the goons began to kick and stomp the shit out of the unconscious man until Rico said that was enough.

"Hold up let me check this nigga's pockets real quick" Rico said as he ran thru the man's pockets until he came across a knot with a rubber band over it. "Aight now get dis mufucka outta here" Rico said as he gave the man one last kick to the ribs.

"Yo grab that fool, and throw him in the trunk" Dred said as he tossed Wolverine the keys to his Lexus.

Once Wolverine got the body out of Rico's presence, Rico noticed Pooky coming his way. Now Pooky was a crack head with all types of schemes up his sleeves. Everybody called him Pooky cause he looked like Pooky from New Jack City.

"What's up Rico?" Pooky said as he reached out to give Rico a pound.

"What's up" Rico said as he left Pooky hanging.

"Yo you think you could hook a brotha up, I've been spending all night with ya'll"

"What you need Pooky?" Rico sighed.

"I got 16 cash and I'm trying to get 2 jumpoffs, come on man you know I'm good for it, I spend wit ya peoples all the time" Pooky whined.

"Aight check it out, I'm in a good mood so I'mma let you slide tonight but next time come wit straight money"

"Rico thank you so much, that's why I only fuck wit you and ya peoples, man cuz ya'll look out for a brotha".

"Look out my ass Nigga" Rico laughed. "Lemme see you do that James Brown dance" Rico, and his whole crew busted out laughing when Pooky broke out into his James Brown slide.

"Aight go in the building and go to the fourth floor staircase B and somebody gonna be waiting there for you"

"Aight Rico good looking out" Pooky said as he disappeared inside the building.

"You too nice to these fiends B" Dred said sitting on the bench next to Rico.

"What you mean, I'm too nice?"

"Man if a fiend can get 16 dollars then he can get 20 dollars" Dred told him.

"You gotta understand their not the fiends, we are" Rico said pointing to Dred and himself. "We fiend for that paper more than they fiend for dat crack"

"You got a good point, I never looked at it like dat" Dred said shaking his head. "But I'm bout to get up outta here and take care of this fool in the trunk" Dred said as he gave Rico a pound and broke out.

"Yeah, I'm about to bounce too" Rico said as he headed home.

***

The next day Rico slept until the sun went down. His sleep was then interrupted by the crackling sounds of a pistol, followed by his phone ringing. "Hello" he answered.

"Yo Rico get downstairs now!" Trina said screaming into the phone.

"I'm on my way" Rico hopped up threw on a T shirt, sweatpants grabbed his four fifth and headed out the door. Once he made it to the front of the building he saw flashing lights and cops everywhere. He then saw Trina coming his way. " Yo what happen?"

"I was chillin on the bench minding my own business when I saw some nigga hop out a car and start dumping on Smoke" she reported.

"Then what happened" Rico asked. "Smoke made it in the building just in time, but before the gunmen could get back to the car J-Murder popped him twice in the back, then Wolverine fired at his man in the driver's seat"

"So them niggas got locked up?"

"Nah they all hopped in Smoke's Benz right before the cops pulled up"

"Damn thats what's up" Rico said pulling out his cell phone. "I want you to go upstairs and keep ya ears open aight? i'm about to call dis nigga Smoke and see what's poppin"

"Aigh't be careful" Trina said kissing Rico on the cheek. Rico then dialed Smoke's number as he watched more police cars pull up on the scene. Smoke finally picked up.

"Yo Smoke what's poppin?"

"Niggaz tried to take me out again, word on da street is that nigga Hollywood got $20,000 on my head" Smoke told him.

"Hollywood who?"

"Some nigga getting money out in LA"

"So get somebody to get at him" Rico said.

"Rico, I don't even know what the fuck he looks like"

"I heard my squad held you down tonight"

"Yeah no doubt J-Murder, and Wolverine saved my life, but yo I think I'm gonna hit up a club downtown tonight, you should roll wit me"

"Yeah I'll fuck wit you tonight just let me know what club you going to and I'll meet you there" Rico said.

"Yeah thats what's up but yo after tonight I'm laying low for a while until I find out some info on dis nigga Hollywood" Smoke said sounding stressed out.

"Yeah I need to get out the hood right now because it's on fire" Rico said. "But yo I'm about to get dressed but I'mma holla at you around 12am"

When Rico stepped off the elevator his cell phone rung once again and when he looked at his caller ID it was Tiffany.

"Hello Rico?"

"Yeah what's up?"

"I'm tryin to see you what's poppin?" Tiffany said.

"I'm gonna hop in the shower real quick then I'm gonna come check you"

"Aigh't call me when your on your way" Tiffany told him before hangng up.

When Rico walked thru the door he saw Kenny sitting on the couch. "Oh what's up, you can't say hi to your uncle no more?"

When Rico looked at Kenny he could tell he was high. In prison he picked up a real bad crack habit. "What's up Kenny?"

"Damn you making money like that?" Kenny grinned. "Making so much money you can't even speak to ya own family?"

"Yo listen B, I just said what's up to you, and all this money shit I don't know what you talking about".

"Bullshit Mufucka everybody knows you fuckin with Smoke now, getting all that real money, you the talk of da projects" Kelly said.

"Yeah whatever" Rico said as he went to his room. The hot water felt good on Rico's body. He stayed in the water for like 45 minutes. Once Rico got out the shower, he threw on his all black Akademics jeans, with his crisp yellow Pittsburgh Pirates fitted hat. Before Rico headed out the door he grabbed $1500 put a rubber band on it and threw it in his pocket. He then grabbed his bracelet and put it on. When Rico reached for his Rolex, he noticed it wasn't where he left it. "Where da fuck is my watch?" Rico said to himself as he searched his whole room. Suddenly Kenny popped into his head. "I know he got my shit" Rico said as he grabbed his four fifth stuck it in his waistband and headed towards the living room. Rico saw Kenny and Janet playing cards. Rico could tell that both of them were blasted.

"Yo Kenny where the fuck is my watch?"

"Watch?" Keeny echoed with a stupid look on his face. "What you talking about?"

"You know what the fuck I'm talking about" Rico said pulling out his four fifth in front of his moms.

"Rico put that gun away" Janet said looking nervous.

"Nah, fuck that I wanna see what this bitch ass nigga gonna do" Kenny said standing up. "Lil nigga I just did 10 years behind the wall with real killers and rapist, what you think I'm scared because you got a lil pistol mufucka?"

"This the last time I'm gonna ask you" Rico said cocking back his pistol. "Where's my fuckin watch, As a matter of fact come outside B" Rico said as he stepped in the hallway.

"Kenny please don't go out there" Janet said trying to hold her brother back.

"Nah fuck that, I'm about to show this nigga what being gangsta is all about" Kenny said as he stepped in the hallway. When Kenny made it to the hallway he didn't see Rico so he made his way to the staircase. Once he opened the staircase door, he saw Rico standing there holding the gun.

"So what you gonna do?" Kenny challenged. Rico looked into Kenny's eyes and his shits looked like 50 cent pieces.

"Damn I don't want to do this" Rico thought as he raised the hammer and pulled the trigger. BOOM! the impact from the bullet sent Kenny flying down the flight of stairs. Rico looked down at Kenny on the pissy staircase ground holding his shoulder. "Listen you bitch ass nigga don't come around here B. next time I see you, your getting bodied" Rico said as he stuck the hot burner in his waistband and spit on Kenny. Rico then flew down the stairs and caught a cab heading to Tiffany's house.

As Rico rode in the cab he saw mad police cars flying past in the other direction. When he knocked on Tiffany's door she answered wearing a big T shirt and some slippers.

"I'm glad you finally made it" she said as she let Rico inside.

"I'm sorry I'm late Ma but I had to take care of something" Rico said looking at Tiffany's thick caramel thighs.

"It's all good I'm just happy you made it" she said as she sat on the couch. "You want something to drink?"

"Yeah let me get some juice" Rico said. When Tiffany left to go get some juice, Rico looked around the apartment. She had a small one bedroom nothing fancy but it was good for her. Rico and Tiffany talked for like two hours before Rico made his move. He leaned over and kissed Tiffany's neck, she let out a soft moan and began to massage Rico's dick. She was pleased when she felt Rico's 9 inch dick begin to rise. Rico then took Tiffany's shirt off and was shocked to see that she had nothing on under her shirt. Rico then placed one of her nice size breast in his mouth and began kissing and sucking on it slow. He then started massaging her clit with his other hand, in a matter of seconds Tiffany's pussy was soaking wet. Tiffany then reached for Rico's belt buckle and noticed the four fifth in his waistband. When Rico saw Tiffany spot his .45 he thought she was gonna spaz out but instead she took the .45 placed it on the coffee table and continued with her business.

"Lay on ya back so I can ride you" Tiffany said with a seductive look on her face. Rico did what he was told and watched as Tiffany climbed on top of him. Rico quickly threw on a condom and went up inside of her.

"Damn she feels so good" Rico thought to himself as Tiffany rode him. Tiffany then planted both feet flat on the bed and started bouncing on Rico's dick. The louder she moaned the more it turned Rico on.

"Turn around" Rico said as he kissed her. When Tiffany got on all fours, Rico couldn't believe how fat her ass was. Rico doved right in. Rico watched as Tiffany's ass clapped up against his torso, as he slid in and out of her nice and slow until he came. Once they finished handling their business they ate some left over Popeye's and passed the blunt back and forth, until they were interrupted by Ricintercom phone.

"Yeah what's good?" he answered.

"You still coming to the club?"

"Definately" Rico replied.

"Bet me, and the whole crew is already here" Smoke informed him. "Make sure you ask for Bobby when you get to the door, Bobby's gonna get you in with ya hammer I already told him you were coming"

"Aight I'm on my way" Rico closed his phone. "Ma I gotta go handle something real quick" he said putting his four fifth back in his waistband.

"Okay be careful out there in the streets" Tiffany said as she walked Rico to the door.

"I'mm'a call you tomorrow aight"? Rico said as he kissed Tiffany on the lips, then turned, and left.

When Rico stepped in the door the club was packed. After about 10 minutes of searching he finally caught up with Smoke and the rest of the crew.

"What's good nigga? It's about time you made it" Smoke said passing Rico a glass of Henny.

"Come on B you know I got business to take care of" Rico said sipping on the Henny. "But fuck all that these hoes in here is looking good" Rico said as him and Smoke hit the dance floor. On the dance floor Rico had his eye on this shorty with the crazy fat ass. She kind of looked like Nia Long. Rico's eyes followed her ass as it moved back and forth to the beat. Once Rico finished his drink he went and got a refill and decided to make his move on Shorty.

"what up Shorty?" he yelled over the blasting music. "I was watching you for a minute and I just had to come and say what's up"

"Oh how sweet" The girl smiled never breaking her two step.

"Everybody calls me Rico" he said extending his hand.

"Okay Rico it's nice to meet you, I'm Kim" she shook his hand.

"Damn Ma I gotta give it to you because your killin that Fendi dress and Ma I'm lovin those Fendi boots"

"Thank you for the compliments but this is my song let me get dis dance" Kim said grabbing Rico's wrist and dragging him to the dance floor. When they reached the dance floor Usher's "Yeah" was bumping through the speakers. Kim was really backing that ass up, Rico had to hang on for dear life as they grinded on one another on the dance floor. Rico and Kim danced for three songs straight before Rico invited her to join him the in VIP section. When they arrived Rico noticed that Kim didn't have anything to drink so he copped a bottle of Moet. As Rico and Kim got to know each other better Nelly's "Get Ya Eagle On" came blasting through the speakers. Rico sat back and watched all the hoes on the dance floor get their eagle on while Kim was talking a whole bunch of nothing in his ear. After Rico's fourth glass of Moet, the flashing lights and the bass from the speakers had Rico feeling good. Kim was just as drunk as Rico and getting hornier by the minute.

"What's good wit This lap dance?" Rico asked.

"Excuse me?" Kim said with a smile. "Your hat is so low I can't even see ya face" Kim said putting Rico's hat on him backwards. "Now what did you say?"

"You think you can handle all this?" Kim asked as she got on top of him straddling her legs on each side of him.

"Ma I know I can handle all this, and some" Rico answered as he gripped Kim's ass with both hands.

"Rico let's get out of here" Kim whispered in his ear.

"Say no more let me holla at my man and let him know I'm out" Rico told her. Rico went and gave Smoke and everybody a pound then, him and Kim broke out and headed to the tele (hotel).

J-Murder and Wolverine sat on the couch in their VIP section watching everybody get their freak on, when they noticed Cali walk up in the club with his main man Hulk. Now Cali was a straight killa from Compton. All he did was get money and body niggaz. He had workers in Queens and in the Bronx getting money for him. He was in town to pick up his money but he wanted to have a good time before he went back to L.A. So he decided to hit up the club before he went back. Now his man Hulk was a beast. He looked like Dee Bo from the movie "Friday" but instead of a bald head he had cornrows going down his back. Hulk didn't play no games, he was about his business. Not only was he Cali's best friend but he was also his bodyguard. The two men walked up in the club glittering, their jewelry was shining so bright that all the bitches were surrounding them at their VIP table, Cali then pulled out a brick of money and copped five bottles of Moet. As the night went on Cali, Hulk, and his flunky's enjoyed themselves. They had the baddest bitches in the club at their table and the bottles kept coming. As Cali sipped on his drink he spotted Smoke over in the VIP section across from him. "I know thats not that mufucka Smoke right here" Cali said to himself as he pulled out his cell phone and dialed Hollywood's number. "What's good this Cali"

" Cali what's poppin my nigga?" Hollywood said blowing out weed smoke.

"Yo you ain't gonna believe who I'm lookin at right now, ya man Smoke"

"Get the fuck outta here, you serious?" Hollywood asked

"Fashizzle" Cali replied.

"Cali I'm gonna need you to take care of that coward for me and since you my man instead of the $20,000 I got on his head I'm gonna give you $50,000"

"Say no more" Cali said quickly hanging up. When Cali hung up his phone he noticed Smoke and Dred getting ready to leave. "Yo Hulk you see that black nigga with the durag on? When he gets outside hit his ass up something real proper, take youngin with you it's about time he got his feet wet, I'm gonna grab these bitches and go to the tele when ya'll finish with that clown come through, and meet me there" Cali said as he grabbed 4 bad bitches and broke out.

"Yo I'm out" Smoke said giving J-Murder and Wolverine both pounds.

"We gonna chill and see if we can slide wit something" J-Murder said giving Smoke and Dred both pounds. When Smoke and Dred made it outside it was drizzling outside. As the 2 men made their way to Dred's Lexus they were stopped by some light skin chick.

"I'm sorry I don't mean to bother you but my friend is feeling you but she's too shy to come over here" the light skin girl said to Dred.

"Yo Ma tell ya friend she ain't got no reason to be shy" Dred said feeling the effect of the liquor. As the two exchanged words they never noticed the all black Acura cruising pass. Hulk held one hand on the steering wheel and the other on his P89.

As Dred continued talking to Shorty he was interrupted by a loud series of gunfire. When he finally realized what was going on he saw Smoke lying in a pool of his own blood.

"Oh shit! Bitch get the fuck out my face" Dred said as he rushed to check on his friend. "Yo dawg hang in there, you gonna make it thru dis" Dred said as he dialed 911. As he looked down at Smoke he noticed he had passed out from all the blood he had lost. When the ambulance finally arrived Dred hopped in his Lexus. "Whoever did dis is gonna pay wit their life" Dred said to himself as he pulled off.

CHAPTER FIVE

As Kenny sat in the hospital nursing his shoulder all he could think about was how he was gonna pay Rico back for popping him in the shoulder. Kenny's thoughts were interrupted when Det. Lance stepped in the room. "Good evening, I'm Det. Lance and you already know why I'm here, do you have anything to tell me?"

"Nah, I ain't telling you shit"

"Listen to me dick head, I looked through your file and I see you just come home and your on parole, now if you don't want to get violated you better let me know something! Two shootings in the projects you live in, in one night you know something mufucka"

"I'm telling you I don't know shit" Kenny said sticking to hiss story.

"Okay how about this, why don't you tell me about your nephew Rico. I hear he's really coming up in the drug game now that he's fucking with Smoke" Det. Lance said.

"I still don't have a clue what your talking about"

In one quick motion Det. Lance pulled out his .357 and back slapped Kenny with it. "Now mufucka you got until the count of three to tell me something or I'm gonna knock every one of your teeth down your throat.

"Alright, alright chill I'll tell you what I know" Kenny said holding the side of his face.

***

With Smoke in the hospital Rico had to step his game up big time in order to help Dred keep the empire running smoothly. Not only was Rico in charge of the projects, he was also in charge of getting the weight to those who needed it. Dred knew Rico would need some form of transportation so he let Rico use the Honda Accord he never drove to conduct business.

In the next month Rico blew up. He copped him another Rolex along with an iced out chain, with a big ass cross flooded with diamonds and on top of that he copped a fully loaded Escalade with 22's on it. Rico even moved into Tiffany's one bedroom apartment with her. He even put a safe in her house. Rico couldn't take living with his mother anymore plus he didn't trust Kenny.

On the other side of town Trina sat in a hotel with some guy she met in the club the other night. Word on the street was he was getting money and lots of it. "So what's up, you gonna talk all night are you gonna come eat this pussy?" Trina asked massaging her clit in front of the stranger. The man immediately took Trina's legs and threw them on his shoulders and dove in face first. The man ate Trina's pussy like his life depended on it. Once Trina got her nut off all the fun and games were over. "Daddy close ya eyes I got a surprise for you" as the man did what he was told Trina grabbed the chrome 9mm from her purse. WHACK!

"Open ya fuckin eyes" Trina said as she bust the man's eye open with the toast.

"Bitch you lost ya fuckin mind?" The man growled.

"Shut the fuck up before I clap ya ass" Trina said taking all the man's money and stuffing it in her purse. "Take off that chain and bracelet"

"Bitch you must be crazy, you gonna have to..." POW! The man's words were cut short as the bullet ripped through his kneecap.

"Okay, okay take everything" the man said tossing all his jewelry to Trina. Trina then grabbed her walkie talkie and told Wolverine to come in. Seconds later Wolverine walked in with a 12 gauge shotgun. "Alright listen up, we can do dis the easy way or we can do dis the hard way, what's it gonna be?"

"The easy way" the man said holding his kneecap.

"I don't want to kill you but if you don't cooperate I will, I'm gonna ask you some simple

questions and I want some simple answers"
Wolverine said walking back and forth. "Now all
you need to do is take me to ya stashn, can you
help me wit that?"

"Yeah I got you just don't kill me"

"Come on dawg I ain't gonna kill you"
(Wolverine lied). Wolverine then duck tapped the
man's hands together and threw him in the trunk.
Him and Trina then hopped in the hooptie and
headed to the address that the man gave them.

***

Kim walked out the beauty parlor looking
like a million bucks. She was feeling good so she
wanted to do something nice for Rico. As she
walked out the beauty parlor she saw Rico sitting
in his truck waiting for her. "Hey Daddy" she said
hopping in the Escalade kissing Rico on the cheek.

"What's good Shorty, I see you lookin like a
brand new woman" he said playfully.

"You know ya bitch gotta stay lookin good
for her boo"

"You better act like you know, but anyway
I'm about to take you home cause I gotta go take
care of some business but be ready later on
tonight cause we going out" Rico said sipping on
some Orange juice.

"Alright I'll be ready but I need to taste you
right now" Kim said unzipping Rico's zipper.

"Yo chill you gonna make me crash"

"Fuck dat I'm not waiting until later" she whined as she threw Rico's dick in her mouth.

"Damn" Rico whispered as he watched Kim's head bop up and down on his shaft. Kim was a pro when it came to sucking dick, she deep throated Rico's dick until he let loose in her mouth. Kim swallowed every last drop. She loved how Rico tasted and every chance she got, she showed him just how much.

"Be ready when I come pick you up" Rico said as he dropped Kim off at her crib. Every since Rico started fucking with Kim he fixed up her two bedroom apartment so when he chilled over there he would be comfortable. After Rico dropped Kim off his cell phone started vibrating, Rico looked and saw it was J-Murder.

"What up?" he answered.

"Your services are needed in the hood right now" J-Murder told him.

"Why what's good?"

"I'll tell you when you get here" J-Murder ended the call.

When Rico pulled up in front of the projects he saw J-Murder and the rest of the crew chilling in front of the building. As Rico made his way to the building he was stopped by his mother.

"Hey Rico where have you been, I've been looking for you" she said.

"I've been busy" he rep,ied flatly.

"Well I need to borrow some money"

"For what, so you can get high? Fuck outta here" Rico said waving her off.

"You got some fucking nerve" Janet said placing her hands on her hips. "For ya information I ain't been high for the last 30 days Mr. Know It All"

"Yeah whatever you look high right now" Rico said as he pulled out a couple of bills out his pocket and handed it to his mother. He knew her history, and it was always the same ole, same ole when it came to her.

"You know what, I don't need ya fuckin money" Janet said throwing the $60 back in Rico's face and walking off. Rico left the money, on the ground, and walked off.

"What's going on around here" Rico said giving J-Murder a pound.

"Shit is crazy around here B this mufucka Pooky called me talking about every time he cops from Stan the shit taste like baking soda so I pressed the nigga Stan and he tried to run, anyway I got the nigga tied up in one of the stash cribs"

"Aight let's go handle this nigga" Rico said as him and J-Murder stepped on the elevator.

"What's up wit Trina and Wolverine?" Rico asked.

"Oh they just finished juxing another one of Trina's vicks (victim).

When Rico and J-Murder stepped in the back room they saw Stan tied to a chair at gun point by Gunner. Gunner was a youngster with a lot of heart. Rico put him on because he reminded him of himself. "So Stan what's up, I hear you wanna be the man?" Rico said pulling out his .45. "I know you ain't smart enough to pull some shit like this on ya own, so who do you work for?"

"Yo Rico please give me another chance...." WHACK!

"Answer the fucking question, who do you work for?" Rico said as he pistol whipped Stan.

"He said he was gonna kill my family" Stan said. "Some cat named Cali"

"So why the fuck didn't you tell me, I could have taken care of dat" Rico huffed.

"No Rico you don't understand, Cali will kill you with out even thinking twice"

"You sound like a fucking bitch" Rico said as he smacked the shit out of Stan. "Where the fuck can I find this nigga Cali?"

"I don't know he only comes to town twice a month and I never contact him he always contacts me" Stan said. "Rico please forgive me, I am sorry" Stan's apology was interrupted when Rico's cell phone rang. Rico looked at his caller ID and saw that it was Goggles. "Yeah what's up?"

"Meet me in front of the building" he said, and nothing more.

"Take this boy to the staircase and kill him" Rico ordered as he went downstairs to meet Goggles.

When Rico stepped out of the building he saw three officers putting Goggles in the back of a squad car. "What the fuck is going on"? Rico thought to himself. Before Rico could walk off he was stopped by Det. Lance.

"Put ya hands behind ya back!" The Detective shouted.

"For what?" Rico resisted.

"Just shut the fuck up and do what I tell you" Det. Lance snarled as he shoved Rico in the backseat and pulled off. When Det. Lance reached Central Park he parked his car and uncuffed Rico. "What the fuck did you bring me to Central Park for?"

"Cause I'm hear to take you to the top"Det. Lance said with a smile.

"Mufucka you can't take me no where cracker!" Rico said purposely trying to insult the detective.

"Okay you wanna play like that, Rico I hear you're the next big thing and I also hear your gun game is serious"

"Okay how much?" Rico said getting straight to the point.

"Twenty thousand a month" Det. Lance said rubbing his hands together. "Listen you help me out, I'll help you out"

"What if I don't want ya help?"

"Rico I'm afraid you have no choice" Det. Lance said smiling. "Either you work for me or you don't work at all"

Rico wanted to kill Det. Lance but he knew he couldn't. In all reality he was in a no win situation.

"Listen Rico it's not as bad as it seems, you don't have to worry about cops harassing you and ya boys no more. If anybody tries to compete with you just let me know and I'll take care of it. Basically I'm letting you get free money, with me on ya team Rico your gonna be untouchable and trust me $20,000 ain't gonna hurt you, now cheer up I gotta go back to the office and take care of some paperwork. I'll contact you next month and let you know where to drop the money off" Det.

Lance said as he hopped in his car and left Rico at Central Park.

Rico hopped out the cab and spotted Trina, Wolverine, and J-Murder standing in front of the building. "What's good B" Rico said giving everybody a pound.

"Same ole shit but what's good wit you, I heard some DT's came and bagged you" J-Murder said taking a long drag on his blunt.

"Yeah somebody put Det. Lance on me"

"Who?" Trina asked.

"I don't know but when I find out I'm gonna catch a case" Rico said seriously.

"So what was Det. Lance talking about?"Trina asked.

"Basically he's muscling me, every month I gotta give that white trash $20,000" As Rico continued talking to his crew a red Blazer pulled up. "Yo ya'll niggas be on point that red Blazer been sitting there for 10 minutes" Rico said with his hand on his hip.

"Oh shit my fault thats my man Lil Foot" Wolverine said as he hopped in the Blazer and made the transaction.

"Yo I gotta go handle something ya'll hold it down out here" Rico said as he hopped in his truck threw on Young Buck's "Straight Outta Cashville"

CD and headed home. When Rico came home he saw Tiffany sitting on the couch wearing some red lace panties and a wife beater. "Hey Baby how was ya day"? Rico asked as he kissed Tiffany.

"It was alright you know same ole disrespectful customers everyday" Tiffany said.

"Baby you know you ain't got to work there any more if you don't want to"

"Yeah I know but I like to have my own money, you know?, but never mind all that, you chilling with me for the rest of the night?"

"Nah I gotta go take care of one more thing but I won't be home late" Rico said taking off his shirt.

"What you taking off ya shirt for?" Tiffany asked smiling.

"You already know what time it is" Rico said as he got butt naked. "Bring dat ass over here" he demanded.Tiffany stepped out of her panties and headed to the bedroom. When Rico arrived in the bedroom he saw Tiffany on all 4's on the bed waiting for him. Rico immediately gripped Tiffany's hips and dove right in. "Who's pussy is dis" Rico asked as he slapped her ass.

"Daddy this pussy is all yours, tear this shit up" Tiffany screamed in extasy. The more Tiffany screamed the deeper Rico went. Rico loved pleasing Tiffany and Tiffany loved when Rico took control. Rico then turned Tiffany on her back and slid in between her legs. Tiffany immediately wrapped her legs around Rico's waist and threw her arms around his neck.

"Fuck me Daddy" she screamed as they came together. Rico then hopped in the shower and let the warm water run down his scratched up back. When Rico got out the shower he threw on his Michael Vick jersey and his Atlanta Falcons hat. "Baby I'll be back in a little while" Rico said kissing Tiffany.

"Aight Baby be careful out there" Tiffany said. When Rico pulled up in front of Kim's crib she stepped out wearing a Christian Dior tube dress with some 3 inch Christian Dior sandals to match. Her dress was so tight it looked like it was painted on.

"What's up Baby" Kim said as she got in the truck and kissed Rico on the cheek.

"Damn Ma you wearing the shit out dat dress" Rico said as he pulled off and headed to the restaurant.

CHAPTER SIX

Cali laid on the bed watching his wife Simone ride his dick. Cali loved when his wife got aggressive with him. Simone was a gangsta bitch and a lady at the same time. She was dark skin with a fat ass and a perfect set of breast with a face that looked like Foxy Brown. Cali made sure she never left the house without her .380. They had been together for seven years but only been married for three years. Simone was ghetto and would do anything for her man and Cali would definitely do anything for his bitch. Cali laid on the bed watching Simone's tits bounce up and down in his face until he was interrupted by his phone ringing. "Hand me dat phone" Cali said with one hand gripped tightly on Simone's fatty. "Yo who da fuck is this?"

"Nigga This is Hollywood"

"Yo how da fuck you get my house number?" Cali asked.

"Don't worry about that" Hollywood spat. "I gave you a fucking job to do and you took my money and you didn't get the job done"

"Yo who the fuck you talking to like that? I did ya punk ass a favor, you fucking faggot don't you ever in ya life talk to me like that!" Cali said hanging up in Hollywood's face.

"Baby is everything alright" Simone asked.

"Yeah Baby it's all good this clown Hollywood acting like he want to go to war"

"He better be easy before he get his wig split" Simone said as ghetto as possible. "I got something that will take your mind off that clown" Simone asked as her head disappeared under the covers.

"Damn baby" Cali moaned as he felt Simone's lips on his dick.

***

"I know this mufucka did not just hung up in my ear" Hollywood said to himself. "Yo Charles round up some soldiers and go take care of that clown Cali. Mufucka think he's the man but what he doesn't know is that in order to be the man you got to beat the man" Hollywood said.

Little did Hollywood know but Cali had already planned on taking over. He already had two cats in Hollywood's organization that was on his team. It was only a matter of time before he took Hollywood out the game. Cali and Simone sat up counting $10,000 that one of Cali's workers had gave him earlier that day. "Baby get me some

Orange juice" Cali said as he slapped Simone on the ass.

"You better stop slapping me like that before you start something you can't finish" Simone said as she put her thong on and headed to the kitchen. Simone returned carrying a glass of Orange juice but before she could even hand him the glass she was stunned when all the lights went out, "Get down" Cali screamed tackling his wife as bullets came flying thi ugh his bedroom window. Once the gunfire stopped Simone reached under the mattress pulled out a 9mm and followed her husband. Cali quickly grabbed his AK from off the top of his dresser and headed towards the hallway. When Cali opened the door he couldn't see shit as him and Simone made their way down the hallway they heard some footsteps coming upstairs. Once the footsteps got closer Cali saw a light and pulled the trigger PAT TAT TAT TAT sending the masked man flying down the stairs, as Cali looked down he saw a flash light on the floor he immediately picked it up and handed it to Simone. "Come on mufuckas" PAT TAT TAT Cali said as he let off a couple of rounds into the ceiling. " Baby go run into the bedroom, grab you some shoes and a jacket and all the money in the safe put it in the duffle bag and hurry up" Cali ordered as he watched Simon's ass jiggle in her thong as she ran in the room.

When Simone made it the room she heard some more gun shots coming from the hallway, she quickly threw all the money from the safe into the duffle bag grabbed some three inch heels her black mink from the closet and made her way back to her husband's side. When she returned she noticed another masked man laid out on the floor and also noticed Cali had a hole in his shoulder. "Baby what happened?"

"I'm alright I just got hit in the shoulder, come on" Cali said as he led the way down the stairs. When they finally reached the bottom of the steps Cali peaked around the corner and saw about 12 infrared dots all over the place. "Aight Baby this is what I want you to do, I'm a turn around and dump on these niggas, I want you to get down as low as you can and run behind the counter" he instructed.

"Aight Daddy you know I'm gonna hold you down" Simone said as she kissed her husband. Cali took a deep breath then turned the corner with his finger on the trigger. PAT TAT TAT TAT as soon as Simone heard the thunderous shots she quickly got low and dashed out from behind the corner. As she was running to the counter Simone heard bullets whistling pass her head. When Cali saw Simone had made it behind the counter he quickly took cover behind the wall. Once Simone got situated behind the counter she peaked around the corner and saw five masked men creeping towards the stairs. Simone quickly aimed her 9mm in the mask man's direction and let off six shots, POW POW POW POW POW POW she hit 4 of the 5 men dead in the chest. The rest of the masked men immediately unloaded on the counter. Once Cali heard Simone's 9mm rang out he sprung from behind the wall and laid every last one of the masked men down. "Baby come on let's get the fuck out of here" Cali said as he took the duffle bag from Simone. Cali made sure the coast was clear before stepping out the front door. "Baby take the car and I'm gonna hop in the truck and I'm gonna meet you at the hotel on Crenshaw" Cali said as he heard the sirens getting closer and closer.

"Aight Baby be careful" Simone said as she hopped in her Land Rover and peeled off. Cali hopped in his Navigator with 22 inch spinning rims and burnt rubber right behind Simone.

***

Rico sat on the bench chilling with Trina and Wolverine just shooting the breeze when he saw Dred coming in their direction. "What's up Baby" Rico said giving Dred a pound.

"Chilling B I just came from the hospital and that nigga Smoke just came out of his coma".

"Word?" Rico said.

"Word to mother son but yo I came to holla at you about something" Dred said.

"Aight what's on ya mind?"

"Yo my man just gave me the word on this nigga Hollywood, I got the nigga address and everything you down to take a trip to Cali with me?" Dred asked.

"No doubt B just let me know when" Rico said excitedly.

"Aight bet we gonna make dis happen in three days"

"Say no more" Rico said as he hit the blunt and passed it to Trina. Rico sat on the bench watching the fiends come and go, he had the hood popping like the playoffs. Rico sat on the bench chit chatting and enjoying his high, when out the corner of his eye he saw Pooky coming his way.

"Rico my man what's going on Baby" Pooky said extending his hand to give Rico a pound.

"What you want now Pooky"? Rico said leaving him hanging.

"I need a favor" Pooky said. "I got $9 cash, what's up I'm trying to get a dime?"

"Pooky you know a blast cost $10" Rico told him.

"Yeah I know but its hard scraping up paper all day, everyday you know what I'm saying?"

"I feel you Pooky, listen I'm gonna hook you up B but don't maknotholesis a habit go in the building and my man is gonna be waiting for you on the 5th floor, "Yo dis nigga Pooky on his way up" Rico said speaking into his walkie talkie.

"Aight" the voice on the other end responded

"Rico I'm starving let's go get something to eat" Trina said as she got up to stretch.

"What you trying to eat?"

"I don't know but I got a taste for some steak" Trina said.

Rico and Trina ended up at I HOPS. As the two enjoyed their steaks Trina's cell phone rang. She talked briefly before hanging up.

"Who was that?" Rico asked.

"That was the white man at the car dealer place, he said I could pick up my new Lexus in two days" Trina said with a bright smile.

"Thats what's up, I see you doing big thangs"

"I try" she said as she sipped her juice. Rico continued eating his steak when he felt his cell phone vibrating, he looked at his caller ID and saw it was Tiffany. "What's up Baby?" he answered.

"I'm sitting in the house missing you Baby?" Tiffany whined.

"I'm in I HOPS right now and as soon as I'm finished I'm coming to the crib"

"Who are you in I HOPS with?" Tiffany asked curiously.

"I'm wit Trina"

"What ya'll out on a date?" Tiffany asked sitting up.

"Come on don't start dat bullshit you know thats my lil sister" Rico remknded her.

"Well I wanna go out tonight too"

"Aight bet I'mma talk to you when I get home" he said quickly ending the call. After their meal Trina and Rico hopped in the Escalade and headed back to the projects. Rico and Trina rode listening to Jay Z when Rico noticed a police car signaling for him to pull over from in his rear view mirror.

"Oh shit the jakes is behind us" Rico said nervously.

"Calm down just pull over and see what they want" Trina said.

"I got the burner on me"

"Give it to me" Trina said pulling Rico's .45 from his waistband and sticking it in her Chanel purse. When Rico pulled over this big red neck cop banged on his window with his flashlight.

"Yes officer, can I help you?" Rico asked rolling down his window.

"Yeah let me see your license and registration" he said shining the bright light in Rico's face.

"May I ask what the problem is?"

"Just do what the fuck I tell you" the cop said in a nasty tone. Right after he said that his partner walked up on the passenger side, Rico handed the officer his license and registration. When the officer returned he asked Rico and Trina to step out of the truck.

"Step out of the car for what?" Rico protested.

"Either get out of the car or I'm gonna get you out of the car" the officer said as he gripped the butt of his .357 get ya fuckin hands on the hood" the officer said as Rico and Trina stepped out of the truck. The officers then cuffed Rico and Trina and made them get on the ground.

"Where did you get a nice truck like this from" the officer said laughing. "What are you a drug dealer?"

Rico remained silent as the officer began to search him. JACKPOT the other officer said as he pulled the .45 out of Trina's purse. "Hey Bob go and check the rest of the vehicle" as he threw Rico and Trina in the back of the squad car. After thirty minutes of searching the two officers finally took Rico and Trina to the police station.

The next morning when Rico was released he went straight to 1 Police Plaza to get all his property. When Rico got released his lawyer told him that Trina's bail was $5,000 and he had to have someone with a job go pay the bail. Rico went downtown got his truck and headed home. When he made it to the crib Tiffany had already left for work. Rico quickly grabbed $5,000 and headed for Mr. Wilson's crib. Now Mr. Wilson was in his forties and he was from the ole school. He even did a bid back in the day. Since he lived next door to Rico's mom he knew Mr. Wilson wouldn't mind doing him this favor. KNOCK KNOCK KNOCK.

"Who is it?" A raspy voice screamed from behind the door.

"It's Rico"

"Hey Rico come on in" Mr. Wilson said letting Rico inside.

"What's up Mr. Wilson?" Rico asked.

"Ain't nothing going on but the rent" Mr. Wilson said laughing. "How can I help you son?"

"I need you to do me a favor, I need you to come downtown with me and bail my friend out of jail"

"Ok no problem you got the money right?" Mr. Wilson asked with a raised brow.

"Yeah I got the money" Rico said as him and Mr. Wilson made their way to the truck. As the two men hopped in the truck, Rico put in Camron's new CD and pulled off.

"This is a nice truck you got here" Mr. Wilson said suspiciously.

"Thank you"

"But you know what you out there doing in them streets is wrong right?" Mr. Wilson said.

"What you mean?" Rico asked keeping his eyes on the road.

"I mean you out there killing your own people and destroying the community with that poison"

"Oh I'm sorry Mr. Wilson but I didn't know the community was so great before crack hit the scene" Rico said sarcastically.

"Thats not what I'm saying, you are destroying the community because the kids look up to you and instead of showing them the right way, you show them the wrong way" Mr. Wilson told him. "If you gon show these kids something, at show them something positive"

"Listen these fuckin crackers ain't giving no young black kids no jobs so thats why I'm here, I'm giving them jobs. I'm putting money in their pockets and clothes on their backs. All I'm tryin to do is help brothas out"

"Rico the only thing you're doing is giving brothas a one way ticket to either the grave or prison" Mr. Wilson said.

"I don't even know why I'm wasting my time talking to this clown, a mufucka like him would never understand why I do what I do" Rico thought to himself as he pulled up to the spot where they held Trina. Forty five minutes later Trina came walking out the front door with a big smile on her face.

"It's about fucking time "she said giving Rico a big hug. "That place is the worst"

"Yeah I know, let's get up outta here" Rico said as they all hopped in the truck. On the ride back Mr. Wilson tried to convince Trina and Rico to turn their lives around. Trina was about to tell the man to shut the fuck up, but quickly decided against it. When Rico finally made it to the projects he gave Mr. Wilson $200 and sent him on his way. Rico hopped back in his truck and was about to head home until he saw Goggles walking up to his truck.

"You know this nigga Smoke home right?" Goggles said with a smile.

"Nah, when he got out the hospital?"

"The nigga got out dis morning, J-Murder tried to call you but he said you wasn't answering the phone" said Goggles.

"Yeah I know when you see that nigga tell him me and Trina got locked up last night" Rico told him, then pulled off.

Married To Da Streets

When Rico made it home he found Tiffany in the bathroom taking a bubble bath. "Hey Baby"

"Don't hey Baby me" she said with an attitude. "Where the fuck were you last night and why was ya phone off?"

"Baby I got locked up last night, me and Trina" Rico told her.

"For what?" Tiffany asked giving him the side eye.

"Cuz I'm black but Trina held it down and took the gun charge for me"

"Come here let me smell ya dick" Tiffany said hopping out the tub dripping wet. As soon Tiffany's hands touched Rico's dick he got brick.

"Now look what you did" Rico said looking Tiffany dead in her eyes.

"Ain't nothing I can't fix" Tiffany said as she sat on the toilet and placed Rico's already hard dick in her mouth and made love to it. She was sucking Rico's dick like she owned it.

"Damn Baby" Rico moaned as he grabbed a hand full of Tiffany's hair. Tiffany sucked her man's dick and put him to sleep. Once Rico was sleep Tiffany cleaned up the house and then joined him.

***

Hulk sat in his 89 Cadillac a block away from Hollywood's crib along with Youngin and two other soldiers. "Yo when this nigga come out make sure ya'll take this niggas legs cause we need him alive" Hulk ordeed as he threw his hoodie on. About 15 minute's later Hollywood step out his crib. Hulk put the petal to the medal, Youngin hung out the window clutching his Uzi along with his two soldiers. Once in striking range Youngin aimed at Hollywood's legs and pulled the trigger. The shots from Youngin's Uzi snapped Hollywood's legs like a twig. When Hollywood's home boys realized what was going on it was too late. Hulk's two soldiers had already opened fire. When Hulk saw Hollywood and his home boys laid out he quickly hit the brakes and hopped out the whip (car). Hulk ran up on Hollywood with his .45 drawn and popped all four of Hollywood's home boys to make sure they were dead.

"What's this all about?" Hollywood asked petrified.

"Shut the fuck up" Hulk said as he threw Hollywood on his shoulder and carried him to the whip. Once Hulk reached the whip he popped the trunk and violently threw Hollywood inside. Hulk hopped in the driver's seat and pulled off.

* * *

Cali sat in his hotel room watching Simone's lips slide up and down on his dick before he was interrupted by his phone ringing. Cali looked at the caller ID and saw that it was Hulk. "What's good?" he answered.

"We got Hollywood over here in Youngin's basement"

"Aight I be there in ten minutes" Cali said ending the call. "Baby we gonna have to finish this later" Cali said pulling up his pants.

"Aight I'm bout to hop in the shower then I'm probably gonna go shopping" Simone said walking to the bathroom wearing nothing but a thong and some high heels.

"I'm bout to bounce you need some money?"

"Nah I'm alright I got about $3,000" Simone yelled from the bathroom.

When Cali stepped inside Youngin's basement he saw a basement full of all his blood niggas. "East Side" he said to all his soldiers and walked straight up to Hulk. "What poppin my nigga?"

"Waiting for you to get here so we could split this niggas wig homie" Hulk replied.

"Yeah we definitely gonna split this niggas wig but first we got to get some info up out this nigga" Cali walked up to Hollywood who was tied up in a chair and could see that Hulk and the rest of his soldiers had beat the shit out of him. "Look at me" Cali said as he slapped the shit out of Hollywood. "Listen I wanna know where all ya stash spots are at and I wanna know where you keep all ya product at"

"I ain't telling you shit" Hollywood said as he started laughing.

"Oh this nigga think I'm playing, yo Youngin let me see that vest you wearing real quick" Cali said taking the vest from Youngin. "I'm gonna ask you one more time where..."

"I already told ya punk ass I ain't telling you shit" Hollywood said cutting Cali's words short.

Cali shook hos head as he placed the bullet proof vest on Hollywood.

"Yo what the fuck you doing" Hollywood said in a panic voice.

"Shut the fuck up" Cali said pulling out his Beretta. POW POW POW.

"You broke my fucking ribs" Hollywood said with tears in his eyes. POW. "Okay, okay I'mma tell you just don't shoot me no more" POW.

"Hurry up I ain't got all day" Cali huffed.

"Alright" Hollywood said begging. After Hollywood told Cali everything he blew his brains out.

"Aight everybody listen up the reason we're all here today is cuz we taking over all of Hollywood spots if ya'll niggas ain't down get the FUCK OUT NOW! After we shut down shit out here, then we going to New York and shut that shit down too! Is all ya'll niggaz ready to ride or what? thats what the fuck I'm talking about let's make dis happen" Cali said to all his soldiers.

CHAPTER SEVEN

Rico sat in the hood watching his team make a killing since it was the first of the month. Rico knew it was gonna be a good day. As him and his crew sat shooting the breeze Rico saw Trina pull up in her new Lexus. Trina hopped out her Lexus with the fresh dubie rocking some low rider jeans with some Gucci sandals with the 3 inch heels.

"What's poppin" Trina said giving the whole crew pounds.

"Damn Trina got the fatty" Rico thought to himself as he gave Trina a pound. "What's good?, I see you doing big thangs"

"You know I gotta keep the rest of them bitches hating" Trina said laughing. Rico was enjoying his day until he saw Harold walking thru the hood.

Rico quickly approached Harold. "Yo what's good you got that paper for me?"

"Nah son you ain't gonna believe what happened some Brooklyn niggaz robbed me son" Harold said.

"Again right?" Rico said in a disbelieving voice.

"Yeah but check this out I'm gonna have all ya money next week".

"You think I'm stupid?" Rico said as he bitch slapped Harold.

"Chill Rico you know I wouldn't do no shit like that, I would steal from my...." Before he could get the chance to spit it out J-Murder dropped him with one punch. As soon as Harold hit the ground Wolverine and the rest of the crew were on him like alley cats.

"Pick this mufucka up" Rico said pulling out his four fifth.

"Chill Rico don't do this, I'mma get ya money" Harold said with tears in his eyes.

"Shut the fuck up and strip" Rico said letting off a shot in the air. Rico then looked to his right and saw all the nosey old ladies from the neighborhood looking in his face. "Yo hurry the fuck up B". Once Harold was butt naked Trina slapped the shit outta him.

"This nigga dick is wild small" Trina said laughing.

"Check this out the next time I see you and you ain't got my money I'm gonna pop ya fucking head off you understand?" Rico said getting all up in Harold's face.

"Yeah I understand" Harold said with tears running down his face.

"Now get the fuck out of here" Rico said as he bust Harold in the back of the head with the burner. After Rico finished humiliating Harold he felt his cell phone vibrating. When he looked at the caller ID he didn't recognize the number. "Yo who this?" he answered.

"It's me Det. Lance"

"How the fuck you get my number?" Rico asked with his face crumbled up.

"Don't worry about it just meet me on 125th and 8the avenue at the Magic Johnson Movie Theatre" Det. Lance ordered. "And make sure you got the money

"Trina you feel like driving me to two fifth?" Rico asked her.

"I don't care" Trina responded.

"Aight let me go get something out my truck" Rico said jogging to his truck. When Rico returned he was carrying a shoe box in a Footlocker bag. Trina and Rico hopped in the Lexus, turned the volume up, and headed to two fifth pumping Shyne's new album. On the ride Rico felt his cell phone vibrating and looked at his caller ID and saw it was Smoke. "What's good my nigga?"

"I'm a little sore but I'll live, but yo I called you cause I'm having a meeting, just you, me, and Dred. So be at the office in an hour" Smoke said.

"Say no more" Rico ending the call. Trina double parked at the Magic Johnson Theatre and let Rico handle his business.

As soon as Rico stepped in the theatre he saw Det. Lance. "What's going on Rico?"

"Same ole shit I can't complain" Rico said dryly.

"Follow me" Det. Lance said leading Rico into the restroom.

"Here take dis paper cause I gotta make moves" Rico said handing Det. Lance the Footlocker bag.

"I'll be in touch around the same time next month, it is nice doing business with you Rico" Det. Lance said with a smirk.

"Yeah whatever" Rico said as he walked out the restroom. "Yo I need you to drop me off back in the hood so I can get my truck" Rico said as he hopped back in Trina's Lex. "Aight" Trina responded as she stepped on the gas.

"What you doing tomorrow?" Trina asked.

"I don't know I'll probably spend some time with Tiffany why what's up?"

"I got another victim for us, he's from North Carolina and he's only here for the weekend to pick up some work so you know he didn't come all this way to New York to cop no peanuts" Trina pointed out.

"Yeah thats what's up, we gonna make dat shit happen tomorrow" Rico said looking at his watch. "But yo what's good wit ya court thang?"

"I gotta go back in 4 months, my lawyer said I'll get a year but I'll only have to do 8 months" Trina said as if it was nothing.

"Good looking on taking that gun charge for me" Rico said.

"It's nothing don't even worry about it" Trina said pulling up behind Rico's truck.

"You a real down ass bitch" Rico said as he hopped out the Lex. "Yo Trina I'mma holla at you later B" he said as he went on about his business.

Rico walked into Smoke's office and gave him and Dred a pound. "So what's up?"

"Well Rico I heard since I got shot you really stepped ya game up" Smoke said looking directly at Rico. "And I want to be the first to let you know that I am proud of you"

"Thats how you do it, one man don't stop no show, get money" he said.

"Now this is how it's going down, this is where me and wifey gonna be staying at for now on. The only mufuckas that know where I live are you two mufuckas and keep it that way. Now for business I want you to keep it how you been doing it". As Smoke was getting ready to end the meeting Dred's cell phone rang.

"Yo I'm gonna take this outside" Dred said as he got up and went in the hallway.

"Yo what's up wit This mufucka, Rico?" Smoke asked suspiciously.

"I don't know" Rico responded with a shrug. Five minutes later Dred came in back in the office.

"Is everything alright?" Smoke asked.

"Yeah everything good" Dred said keeping his answer short, and sweet.

"I'mma get up outta here to B" Rico said giving Smoke a pound. "Okay Baby you be cool" Smoke said as he watched Rico, and Dred exit his office.

When Rico stepped in the crib he noticed that Tiffany had just got her hair done. "Hey Baby ya dubie is looking right" Rico said as he kissed her.

"You know I gotta stay fly for my hubby" Tiffany said smiling.

"That's what I like to hear, now get dressed I'm taking you out"

"Where are we going?" Tiffany asked excitedly.

"I'm going to take you to the movies to see that new shit, you wanted to see then after that we gonna go to dinner, now hurry up and get dressed" Rico said as he slapped Tiffany on the ass. When Tiffany stepped out the bedroom she had on a skin tight Chanel dress with the matching sandals with the three inch heels.

"Come on let's go and you driving too" Rico said tossing Tiffany the keys. After the movie Tiffany headed back to the V (vehicle) but before they reached the whip Rico heard somebody shout out "Damn Shorty got the fat ass" when Rico looked up he saw some clown ass nigga with mad jewels on sitting on the hood of a Cadillac.

"Rico just ignore that nigga" Tiffany said as she grabbed Rico's hand. Rico was about to let it go but then but then he thought about it, and pulled out the heat and made a U turn. "You see something you like over there money?" Rico said as he walked up on the guy. Before the guy could answer Rico knocked both of his front teeth out with the burner. "Get up you fucking faggot" Rico said grabbing the man's braids. "Take all dis shit off" Rico said as he took the man's rings, chain, bracelet, watch, and earrings. "What else you got for me" Rico said as he bust the man in the head with the burner again.

"Rico thats enough" Tiffany yelled from the sidelines.

"Nah fuck that I'm gonna teach this nigga some fucking manners, matter of fact give me all ya money and strip" Rico said. The man tossed Rico a stack of money with two rubber bands around it and got butt ass naked.

"Now apologize to my Queen you bitch ass nigga" Rico sticking the burnet to the man's ribs.

"Ms. I'm sorry I apologize for disrespecting you"

"Now when ya friends ask you who did this to you, make sure you tell them Rico did it, now get the fuck out of here" Rico said dismissing him with a shove. As the man jogged down the block butt naked Rico pointed his four fifth at the man's ass and pulled the trigger once the man collapsed he grabbed Tiffany's hand and power walked to the truck.

"Aight now let's go get something to eat" Rico said as he pulled off.

"Rico you need to learn to control ya temper" Tiffany said looking Rico dead in his face.

"That clown got what he deserved, anybody who tries to disrespect you is gonna get it straight like that" Rico said as he stopped at the red light.

"I understand what your saying Rico but you went to far back there, what if you would have gotten locked up over that bum ass nigga, then what?"

"Yeah maybe I did go too far tonight but I bet that nigga won't do no dumb shit like that again" Rico said as he turned the volume up and blasted " Da Westside Story" by Game. As him and Tiffany headed to the restaurant.

***

J-Murder sat on the bench with thirty mufuckas from the hood around him. He and Wolverine made sure everything was running smoothly before they entered the dice game. Trina sat on the bench watching the dice game, when she looked up she noticed four men wearing hoodies coming in her direction. "Ya'll get on point" Trina said pulling her 9mm out her hand bag. The four men with hoodies stopped dead in their tracks and hit a U turn and started walking in another direction. As Trina watched the men change direction she heard Goggles over the walkie talkie. "Yeah what's poppin" she answered.

"Yo four niggas wearing hoodies just jacked us and they shot me and two other workers". Once Goggles said that Wolverine and J-Murder both heard it over their walkie talkie.

"There them niggas go right there!" Wolverine said as he pulled out two Berettas and let off four shots. When the four men heard the shots all four of them immediately turned around and opened fire with their Mac 10's TAT TAT TAT TAT Trina ducked behind the bench and threw five shots back at them. The four men let off a couple of more rounds and hopped in the Blazer and pulled off. Before the Blazer got out the hood J-Murder shot out its back window.

"Bitch ass niggaz..... yo Goggles" J-Murder yelled through his walkie talkie.

"Yeah" he responded weakly.

"What floor you on?"

"Seventh" Goggles told him.

J-Murder called a ambulance, as everyone split up. Trina hopped in her Lex and hit the Westside Highway. "Rico gonna flip the fuck out when he hear about this shit" Trina thought to herself as she picked up her cell phone and dialed Rico's number.

Rico and Tiffany stepped off the elevator and headed down the hallway towards the apartment. As they walked down the hall Rico saw Tiffany's ass bouncing from side to side in her Chanel dress. " I'mma bust her ass" Rico thought to himself as they entered the apartment. "Yo come here" Rico said grabbing Tiffany by the arm. "You still mad at me Baby?"

"No I ain't mad at you I know you were just trying to protect me" she said.

"Baby I would go crazy if anything ever happened to you" Rico said warmly.

"I know you would thats why I love you so much"

"Girl you just love me for my doggystyle" Rico said smiling.

"Ya doggystyle?" Tiffany echoed. "Nigga please"

"Oh so you don't love my doggystyle?" Rico asked cupping Tiffany's ass cheeks in his hands.

"You know I love ya doggystyle" Tiffany said throwing her tongue in Rico's mouth. Tiffany then hopped up on Rico and wrapped her legs around his waist. Rico carried her into the bedroom and laid her down on the bed.

"Daddy let me see what that doggystyle is all about" Tiffany said as she hopped out of her dress.

"Keep those heels on" Rico said as he stripped. Once he was naked he saw Tiffany in the bed on all fours wearing nothing but her heels. "Come here Baby" Rico said as he entered Tiffany from the back nice and slow.

"Ahh Daddy" she moaned softly. The more Tiffany moaned the deeper Rico went until he finally came. Rico laid on the bed while Tiffany went to the bathroom to wash her booty. As Rico laid on the bed he heard his cell phone vibrating on the dresser. He looked at the caller ID and saw dat it was Trina again. "What's good Ma?"

"Where you at?"

"I'm in the crib, what's up?" Rico noticing the seriosness in Trina's voice.

"I'll be there in five minutes make sure you dressed" then the line went dead.

"Baby I'll be right back" Rico said as he kissed Tiffany and put his .45 in his waistband.

Rico was standing in front of his building when he saw Trina pull up in her Lexus. "What the fuck is going on?" Rico asked hopping in the whip.

"Somebody just hit us up" Trina just came right out with it.

"How much did they get from us?"

"Fifteen thousand and they clapped Goggles, and Pee Wee, and Dee both got bodied"

"Damn Pee Wee was just 16 years old" Rico said putting his head down.

"Yeah I know" Trina said as she stopped at the red light.

"Call everybody from the crew and tell them to meet us at the stash crib in the Bronx" Rico said as he pressed play on the CD player. Trina and Rico rode listening to D Block for the rest of the ride.

When Trina and Rico walked in the stash crib they were surprised to see the whole crew there waiting for them.

"What happened tonight?" Rico asked. Everybody remained silent. "So don't nobody know nothing?" Rico said sounding like Nino Brown.

"We was rolling dice when I heard Goggles over the walkie talkie, talking about four niggaz just popped him and two other workers and took everything they had" J-Murder said loading his .45.

"So ya'll just let these mufuckas come and take all our shit?"

"By the time we realized what was going on they were already in the truck" Wolverine said.

As Rico sat down thinking of what to do he felt his cell phone vibrating. "Who the fuck is this Rico answered without looking at the caller ID.

"Rico, it's me Pooky"

"What the fuck you want Pooky?" Rico said not in the mood to talk to the fiend.

"I think I might be able to help you out" Pooky said.

"How?"

"Cause I know who hit ya spot up tonight"

"Who?" Rico asked standing to his feet.

"Kenny" Pooky announced.

"My uncle Kenny?" Rico asked. "How the fuck you know?"

"Cause I was there.... I had just got off the elevator on the 7th floor when I heard the gunshots, after I heard the shots I looked through the staircase window and saw Kenny and three men wearing hoodies. I thought if they saw me they would probably shoot me too so I hopped back on the elevator and broke out" Pooky reported.

"So how do you know it was Kenny for sure?" Rico asked, he needed to be sure the info Pooky was giving him was correct.

"Cause I smoked with him a few times and I never forget a face"

"Aight good looking Pooky, If you hear anything else make sure you let me know"

"Uhm Rico you gonna hook me up for this info right?"

"Yeah I got you Pooky, be easy" Rico said hanging up in the fiends ear. "Yo I just got word dat Kenny and some of his boys he did time wit hit us up" Rico said walking back and forth. "Now something like this can never happen again, ya'll mufuckas is getting paid to much money to be letting shit like this happen, especially you mufuckin lookouts ya'll on them rooftops all fucking day if something don't look right get on the walkie talkie and say something so Wolverine and the rest of the gang can handle it"

"So what's up, what you want us to do about Kenny?" Wolverine asked ready to put in some work.

"Don't worry about that I'll take care of it" Rico responded.

"You got all these soldiers around you, you need to start putting them to work cause the only thang thats gonna happen is you gonna fuck around and catch a case" Trina said while fixing her hair in the mirror.

"I know you care about me and everything Trina but I gotta handle this myself, now tomorrow I want a few of you to go wit Trina and take care of this down south nigga, I gotta make moves right now" Rico said giving everybody a pound. " Yo Trina after all ya'll handle that business hit me up and let me know how everything went down aight"

"I got you"

"Aight bet ya'll niggas hold it down" Rico said as he caught a cab and headed home.

***

CHAPTER EIGHT

The next morning Dred sat in Starbucks waiting for his guests to arrive. Ten minutes later Cali and Hulk walked in.

"My main man Dred, what's poppin?" Cali said giving Dred a pound.

"I'm chillin what took you so long to get here?"

"I had to take care of something real quick but fuck that let's talk business. I hear you out here doing ya thang in the big city. My man has been watching you for a while now and he tells me you would fit perfectly in my organization, my man also tells me you have a partner you trying to get rid of, so what's up wit that?"

"Well it's just like I told you over the phone, I could make more money wit Smoke outta the picture and plus the nigga tried to play me. I been fucking wit this nigga from the beginning then this young mufucka Rico comes along and, Smoke just straight up puts him on, the nigga ain't put in no work or nothing so fuck it! If it's fuck me then it's fuck you" Dred said taking a sip of his coffee.

"Yeah I been hearing a lot about this Rico cat, I heard the nigga is about business" Cali said.

"Man that nigga ain't about franks" Dred hated.

"Aight so I tell you what I'mma do" Cali said sipping on his Orange juice. "I'mma take care of this nigga Smoke for you, and since you hate Rico so much I'mma let you take care of him. Once Smoke and Rico are gone I'mma have my workers take care of everything and all you gotta do is sit back and get paid I guarantee you'll make twice as much money fucking wit me then you made you made fucking wit Smoke. And you ain't even gotta worry about no drama cause with this thang right here" Cali said revealing the butt of his 9mm, "I shoot betta then Jordan"

"Damn dats a big mufucka" Dred said to himself as he looked at Hulk. "Aight so I guess we got ourselves a deal, just let me know when you gonna body that nigga Smoke" said Dred.

"You got a address for me?"

"Yeah I got it right here" Dred said handing Cali the paper with the address on it.

"Aight so I'm gonna make this happen ASAP once thats done I'll contact you" Cali said as him and Hulk made their exit.

***

Rico sat in Kim's crib listening to the new Jim Jones album waiting for his food to be ready. About ten minutes later Kim walked into the living room wearing nothing but a thong and some slippers carrying Rico's plate. "Here I made you some French toast, eggs, and turkey sausage"

"Thanks baby" Rico said as he dug into his food. After Kim finished washing the dishes she came back in the living room wearing a big t- shirt. "So what's up you chillin wit me today or what?" She asked sitting next to Rico on the couch.

"Yeah I'm chillin with you today why what's up, you wanna go somewhere?" he asked.

"Nah I just wanna chill in the crib today"

"Aight bet cause I'm about to take a nap" Rico said as he stretched out on the couch and placed his head in Kim's lap and dozed off. When Rico woke up he looked up and saw that Kim was still sleeping. As Rico got up to go brush his teeth he felt his cell phone vibrating. Rico looked at the caller ID and saw that it was Tiffany calling from her cell phone. "What's up?"

"Hey Baby it's me what you doing?" Tiffany asked.

"Chilling about to get something to eat why where you at?"

"At work on my break, I get off in two hours you gonna be home when I get there?" she asked.

"Yeah I'mma be home and bring me some chicken when you come home"

"I got you" Tiffany chuckled. "I'mma see you when I get home cause my break is over"

"Aight Baby I'll see you at the crib...one" As Rico was peeing Kim walked into the bathroom and started brushing her teeth. "Yo I gotta get up outta here and take care of something" Rico said walking out the bathroom. "Yo I'mma call you later on aight?"

"Alright but you know you can't leave wit out breaking me off" Kim said sitting on the couch and at the same time pulling Rico's dick out. "Uhm" she said as she placed Rico's already hard dick in her wet mouth and began to stroke it. "Damn" Rico moaned grabbing a hand full of Kim's hair and started fucking her mouth like it was a pussy.

"Uhm, uhm" Kim moaned as she let the juices from her mouth run down her chin and neck. Rico continued to fuck Kim's mouth until he finally exploded.

"Who's ya bitch" Kim asked as she wiped her mouth.

"You know you my bitch" Rico said as he kissed Kim on the cheek.

"You be safe out there and call me later" Kim said as she watched Rico walk out the front door.

Tiffany walked in the crib with her dubie pinned up and saw Rico sitting on the couch playing Madden. "How you feel baby" Tiffany asked kissing Rico on the lips.

"I'm good Ma what's up wit you, you look tired"

"I am" Tiffany said taking off her shoes and sitting next to Rico.

"Fuck that my wife ain't gonna be busting her ass at no mufuckin Popeye's, starting tomorrow you no longer work there. I don't even know why you wasted ya time there anyway I already told you, you ain't gotta work no more" Rico said massaging Tiffany's feet.

"I know I ain't gotta work but I like to get my own" Tiffany said.

"Aight so I tell you what, you take a week and just relax and figure out what you wanna do and we gonna make it happen aight" Rico said.

"Okay baby I'ma just relax for a week and get my mind right. But first I'ma hop in the shower and get out these clothes"

"You need some help wit that?" Rico asked.

"Yeah I think I could use another hand" Tiffany said walking towards the bathroom with a smirk on her face. Once Rico hopped in the shower he heard his cell phone ringing, he looked at his caller ID and saw that it was Trina. "Holla at ya boy"

"We just finished hitting this down south nigga up" she told him.

"What ya'll get him for?"

"We caught the nigga right before he was going to re-up, the mufucka had $ 150,000 in a duffle bag in his truck. I gave Wolverine and Gunner $ 20,000 a piece, I put $ 20,000 up for J-Murder, I took $ 45,000 and I got $ 45,000 for you"

"That's what I'm talking about, thats a good look right there" Rico smiled.

"I'mma try to hit the club tonight, what's good you rolling?"

"Yeah I'm about to get dressed right now, I'll meet you at the projects in an hour" Rico threw on his yellow Timbs, some black jeans, his purple Randy Moss jersey along with his Minnesota Vikings fitted. "Yo Ma I'll be back later on" Rico said kissing Tiffany's lips.

"Where you going?" Tiffany asked putting on her baby face.

"I'm going to the club"

"Aight you be careful and don't be all up in no bitches face"

"Stop acting like that Ma you know I love you" Rico said.

"Yeah I know Daddy go have some fun, I'll be here waiting for you when you get back"

"Aight Baby I won't be back late" Rico said walking out the door.

When Rico pulled up in front of his mom's building he saw Trina, Wolverine, and J-Murder all dressed to impress. "What's good ya'll ready to make moves?"

"Yeah nigga we been waiting for you" Trina said handing Rico the book bag that held the $45,000 inside.

"Aight let's be out" Rico said as all four of them hopped in their own whips. When Rico and the crew arrived at the club they saw that the line was around the corner.

"Damn look at those bitches on line" J-Murder said putting a piece of gum in his mouth. Fortunately Trina knew the bouncers at the door and they let Trina and her friends in with out waiting on line. Once Rico stepped in the club he felt all eyes on him. It seemed like every gold digger in the club had they eye on Rico and his crew and he couldn't blame them cause he was glittering. The iced out cross on his chest bounced every time he took a step. Rico and his crew made their way straight to the bar, they all copped a bottle and headed straight to the VIP section. Rico sat with a drink in his hand bobbing his head to the music along with Trina, while J-Murder and Wolverine hit the dance floor and got their groove on. As Rico sat sipping on his drink he saw this shorty that favored Beyonce with the crazy fat ass. From the way her ass jiggled in her stretch pants Rico could tell she didn't have any panties on. As Rico continued to watch her ass bounce up and down the woman looked Rico's way and caught him looking at her ass. At first Rico thought the girl was gonna say something but instead she just gave him a little smirk.

"Come here Ma" Rico yelled over the blasting music. When Shorty made her way to the VIP section Rico liked what he saw, Shorty was definitely a dime. "What's poppin Ma, I noticed you ain't have a drink in ya hand, what up wit that?"

"I ain't tryin to get all drunk tonight"

"Yo Ma stop frontin and have a seat". Once the girl sat down Rico handed her a glass of Belve. "Yo I'm Rico" he said extending his hand.

"I know who you are" she said as she shook his hand.

"Oh really?"

"Yeah I heard about you" the chick said.

"All good things I hope?" Rico smiled.

"Yeah nothing bad"

"So Ma, what's ya name?"

"My friends call me Peaches" she told him.

"Ok Peaches it's nice to meet you" Rico and peaches sat and got to know each other a little better as the night went on. As Rico sat talking to Peaches he saw some skinny kid carrying a bottle of Moet walking up to VIP. Rico immediately placed his hand on the handle of his four fifth. "What's good money?"

"Yo fams my man told me to bring you this bottle" the man said.

"Ya man, who the fuck is ya man?"

"My man right there" the skinny kid said pointing to some nigga in a VIP section on the other side of the club.

"Fam check this out, I don't want no bottle from you or ya man, as a matter of fact get the fuck up outta here" Rico said as he mushed the skinny kid. "What the fuck is wrong wit that clown" Rico said giving Trina a pound.

"I don't know but he better be easy before he get his melon touched" Trina said sipping on the bubbly. Rico and peaches continued exchanging words at this point both of them were saucy (drunk).

"Oh thats my shit" Peaches screamed as "All About the Benjamins" came blasting through the speakers. "Come on let's dance" Peaches said dragging Rico on to the dance floor. Rico and Peaches grinded for three sons straight until Rico felt somebody tapping him on the shoulder. When he turned around he was face to face with the nigga that sent him the bottle of Moet. "Can I help you?"

"Let me holla at you for a second" the man said with a mouth full of gold teeth.

"Aight step into my office" Rico said as he led the man to his VIP section and offered him a seat and a drink. "So what's up"? Rico asked sizing the man up. The man wore shoulder length dreds and mad jewels.

"Well first of all Rico my name is Buck and I been hearing a lot about you. I'm from Atlanta and I got a lil something poppin out there but I ain't doing it big like you but anyway to make a long story short I been hearing about you and how you get down and I wanted to know how could I get down wit ya team?"

Rico sipped on his drink. "What can you bring to the table?"

"Well I got a lil something going on in the Bronx but the thing is ain't really got enough work to do it big like I want but it's this abandon building in Hunts Point that I had my eye on. We could really shut shit down, all I need is a lil help from you" Buck said turning up the bottle of Moet.

"You look like you got ya head on your shoulders so I tell you what I'm gonna do, I'ma set you up with everything you need but since I don't know you like that I'ma have a few of my wolves go over there with you until we get to know each other better, you know what I'm saying?"

"Yeah I respect dat but I was thinking we could put four look outs on the roof of the abandon building?"

"Yeah we could definitely do that and we gonna make sure everybody keeps a walkie talkie on them at all times" Rico told him.

"I just wanna thank you for giving me the opportunity to do my thang how I been tryin to do it" Buck said sipping on the bubbly.

"What's good everything alright over here?" J-Murder stated plainly.

"Yeah everything good Buck this my man J-Murder, J-Murder this is Buck" Rico said introducing the two.

"Aight I got this honey over there waiting for me I just came to make sure everything was good" J-Murder said heading back to the dance floor. Rico and Buck continued discussing business until they were interrupted by Trina.

"Damn these niggas in here is thirsty" Trina said taking a seat next to Rico.

"Trina this is Buck and Buck this is Trina" before Rico could finish introducing the two Peaches was dead in his face.

"What's good Rico you forgot about me or something" she said with the puppy look on her face.

"My fault I had to take care of something real quick" Rico said as him and Peaches went back to the dance floor.

As Buck sat in the VIP section sipping his bottle of Moet he had his eye on Trina. The way her ass moved to the beat had him hypnotized. "Shorty got it going on, fuck that I'm going to get me a dance" Buck said to himself as he got up and approached Trina. "What's up Ma? Why don't you show Buck what you working wit"

Trina obeyed and threw the ass back at Buck. Buck held on to Trina's hip with one hand and held his bottle with the other as Trina grinded her ass all over Buck's dick to her favorite reggae song. After the two finished dancing Buck led Trina to the bar so he could get her another drink.

"So how long you been in New York?" Trina asked while waiting for her drink.

"I been here for about a year but I been on some back and forth shit you know?"

Married To Da Streets

"Yeah I feel you" As Trina turned around with here drink in her hand some drunk ass nigga bumped into her causing her to spill her drink all over her new Prada dress.

"Damn bitch watch where the fuck you going" the man said angrily.

"Who the fuck you talking to?" Trina asked placing her hands on her hips.

"Oh what we got a problem?" The man said lifting up his shirt and revealing the butt of his .357 before Trina could respond Buck bust the guy in the head with a Moet bottle. As soon as the man's body hit the wet floor Trina immediately grabbed the man's .357 from his waistband and joined Buck and started stomping the man. Seconds later three big bouncers came and broke up the fight and threw Trina and Buck out the club. Once outside the club Trina and Buck made their way to Trina's Lexus.

"You got a ride home?" Trina asked.

"Yeah my whip is down the block, I just wanted to make sure you made it to ya whip okay" Buck said staring Trina dead in her eyes.

"Damn this nigga is sexy as hell" Trina thought to herself looking at Buck's crotch. "What's up you wanna go get something to eat?"

"Yeah Shawty, I'm starving but everything is closed this time of night so what you wanna do? you know how to cook?" he asked.

"Of course" Trina answered.

"So what's up you wanna come to my crib and hook something up?"

"I'm down"

"Cool I'ma go get my whip from down the block" Buck said walking down the block.

As Trina sat waiting for Buck to come back she noticed the man who she got into it with exiting the club with a few of his homeboys. Trina immediately pulled her 9mm from her Prada bag and waited to see how things played out. A few seconds later up in his 89 Malibu with 20 inch chrome rims.

"What it is folk?" Buck yelled stepping out of his whip clutching his P89 Rugar. Once Trina saw Buck back out on the clowns she hopped out her whip holding her 9mm and held him down. Once shit was about to pop off Trina saw Rico coming out the club with Peaches.

"A yo Frank what the fuck are you doing?" Rico asked.

"Yo B I'm bout to give it to this bitch and her man" Frank growled.

Rico looked across the street and saw Trina and Buck. "Yo thats my lil sister right there B."

"Oh my fault Rico I swear I didn't know". Frank was the average hustler, every week he copped 200 grams from Rico, he knew he fucked up now.

"Yo son you gonna pop my sister B.?" Rico asked seriously.

"Yo I swear I didn't...." Before he could get the words out Rico had stole on him. "Yo Frank don't ever let nothing like dis happen again B. Yo we all on the same team let's get this money"

"No doubt B my fault man this shit will never happen again, you got my word" Frank said giving Rico a pound.

Rico and Peaches made there way across the street to where Trina and Buck stood. "Yo everything good?"

"Yeah I'm fine" Trina answered. "That clown was gonna pop me if Buck didn't come through and hold me down"

"Good looking I owe you one" Rico said giving Buck a pound.

"Don't worry about it it's nothing, I do this for a living" Buck smiled.

"Me and Peaches gonna go take care of some unfinished business" Rico stated as he walked off with one hand on Peaches's ass.

"What's up, you ready to make this happen?" Buck asked.

"Let's do this" Trina said as she hopped in her Lexus and followed Buck to his crib.

***

Cali and Youngin stood staked out in front of Smoke's crib. "Damn where the fuck This nigga at cuz, we been waiting here all day" Cali stated plainly.

"Don't worry he gotta come home sometime" Youngin said.

"Yeah and I'ma light his ass up for making me wait all mufuckin day" Cali said loading his Uzi.

On the other side of town Smoke and his wife Jessica were on their way home from a four day vacation. "Did you enjoy ya vacation?" he asked.

"Yeah it was nice but I can't wait to get home" Jessica answered.

"Don't worry Baby we will be home in a minute" Smoke said stepping on the gas. Smoke pulled up in his driveway and placed the Range Rover in park.

"Baby grab these bags for me, you know I can't carry those bags by myself Smoke" Jessica said removing bags from the back seat.

Once Cali spotted Smoke he couldn't wait to merk (kill) him. "Yo let's do this" Cali said hanging out the sun roof clutching his Uzi. As Smoked helped Jessica with the bags he noticed a black Jetta cruising by before he realized what was going on he saw a hooded man aiming an Uzi in his direction. Smoke immediately dropped his bags and reached for his Desert Eagle but before he could pull it out he heard the Uzi spit PAT TAT TAT TAT TAT. Instead of pulling his Desert Smoke turned and tackled Jessica and shielded her with his body. As Jessica screamed Smoke could feel the bullets rip through his back. Once the shots rang out Jessica heard tires screeching as she turned over and saw Smoke laid out full of holes the only thang she could do was scream and call 911.

CHAPTER NINE

Rico sat in his bed playing Madden while Tiffany was giving him some good top. Tiffany owned Rico's dick and every time she gave him head she let it be known who his wife was. She was flyer then any other bitch and she knew it. The difference between her and other bitches was Tiffany really loved Rico and would do anything for him. Other bitches just wanted Rico because he was shining. Rico did a good job keeping his other bitches a secret cause if Tiffany found out he was fucking somebody else all hell would break loose. Rico knew Tiffany had a crazy side to her but he hoped to stay on her good side. It was funny to Rico cause he knew if he even thought Tiffany was fucking around on him he was going to catch a body. Rico sat watching his wife's head move to a rhythm until he was interrupted by a series of knocks at the front door. "Yo go see who's knocking like the boyz (cops)"! Rico said cocking his four fifth. Tiffany ran back into the room looking startled.

"Its the cops!, it's like four of them crackers wearing suits" Tiffany said with a scared look on her face.

"Aight be easy they don't have a warrant cuz if they did they would have kicked the door in" Rico said handing Tiffany three burners (guns). Tiffany ran in the kitchen with her ass jiggling all over the place in her thong. She ran in the bedroom and threw some sweatpants on as the knocking got louder and louder.

"Yeah can I help you?" Rico asked cracking the door.

"Yeah I'm looking for Rico Anderson" the cracker said trying to look inside the house.

"Yeah I'm Rico what's the problem?"

"We just want you to answer a few questions"

"Questions about what?" Rico asked.

"Motherfucker I ain't got time for all these games" the cracker said as he pushed his way into the door and pulled Rico into the hallway and cuffed him.

"I want to see all ya warrants" Tiffany yelled as she ran into the hallway.

"Ms. Go back in the house this doesn't concern you" one of the detectives yelled.

"I hate you fuckin crackers" Tiffany stated as she watched the detectives escort Rico down the hall.

"Baby call my lawyer for me!" Rico yelled as the detectives escorted him down the stairs.

"Baby don't worry about nothing, I'll have you out by the morning" Tiffany said as she watched the detectives disappear into the staircase with her man.

Once the jakes were gone Tiffany ran in the crib picked up the house phone and called J-Murder. On the fourth ring he finally picked up. "Hello"

"Yeah what's up this Tiffany"

"Oh what's poppin Tiff?"

"The cops came and took Rico"

"Why did they take him?" J-Murder asked.

"I don't know, I'm about to run to the station and find out"

"Did they have warrants?"

"Nah they didn't have shit they just came and took him" Tiffany said talking in a fast pitch tone.

"Aight this what I want you to do, go to the station and when you find out what's up hit me back"

"Aight I was just calling to let you know what was going on just in case they came looking for you next" she said.

Tiffany took a quick shower and got dressed. She threw on some knee high Gucci boots with some jeans a wife beater and some Gucci shades. She walked out the door taking her dubie out as she headed to her whip. When Tiffany got outside she hopped in her 2009 red Charger, the sun beamed off her 20 inch chrome rims as she pulled off pumping Mary J Blige.

When Rico got to the police station he was escorted to the interrogation room.

"Have a seat Mr. Anderson" the detective said pulling out a chair for Rico to sit in. "Do you know a gentleman by the name of Shawn Givens?"

"Nah I never heard of him" Rico yawned.

"In the streets they call him Smoke" The detective said.

"Nah I don't know who your talking about" Rico lied.

"Listen Mr. Anderson we know that you and Smoke are partners so stop bullshitting us"

"I'm sorry but I have no idea what ya'll are talking about" he said sticking to his story.

"Listen dip shit Smoke got murdered two days ago and me and my partner got a strange felling that whoever murdered him is coming for you next". Rico's heart dropped when he heard Smoke had been killed but still he had to play dumb. "Listen detectives I don't know any of these people you are talking about, if I could help you I would but I can't"

Det. Ford had heard enough he went and got all up in Rico's face. "Listen cocksucker you might think your slick but around here nobody is greaser than me. I am as slick as they come mufucka. You fucked up this time cause now I'm gonna be on ya ass. Now get the fuck outta here before I beat the living shit out of you" Det. Ford said before he walked out the interrogation room.

When Rico made it to the lobby he saw Tiffany sitting on the hard bench waiting for him. "Hey Daddy" she said jumping into Rico's arms.

"How you feeling Ma?"

"Better now" she said planting wet kisses all over his face. Once they got back to the whip Tiffany threw on Mary J Blige and pulled off.

"Let's go to I HOPS, I'm hungrier then a hostage" Rico said pushing his seat back as far as it could go.

"You tired Baby?" Tiffany asked.

"Word wake me up when we get there"

When the two finished their meals Rico pulled out his cell phone, and made a call.

"Det. Lance please?"

"This is Det. Lance speaking who is this?"

"Rico"

"Hey Rico what's going on I wasn't expecting to hear from you until next week"

"Listen I ain't got time to be playin games, you told me if I paid you every month I wouldn't have to worry about me or my crew getting harassed"

"Calm down what are you talking about?" Det. Lance asked.

"What am I talking about, I gave you $ 60,000 cash so far and within these three months, I've been arrested twice and my crew is being fucked over as well" Rico complained.

"Rico first of all watch your tone when you talk to me, second of all who's been harassing you?"

"Some faggot named Det. Ford"

"Det. Ford damn that mufucka must have just gotten back from his vacation, he's a real goody two shoes Robocop mufucka" Det. Lance huffed. "We gonna definitely have to do something about him, i tell you what just try to stay out of trouble for awhile until I get everything under control. I'ma call you next week to let you know where to meet me with that paper so when we meet up I'll have something figured out"

"Yeah you better cause I ain't got time for this bullshit" Rico barked.

"I hear you give me a week and I'll have everything figured out"

When Rico got off the phone Tiffany paid the bill and her and Rico headed back to the whip. "Yo take me to the projects real quick I gotta holla at J-Murder about something before we go back to the crib". Tiffany obeyed and made a detour to the projects. Tiffany double parked and beeped the horn. When J-Murder and Trina saw the Charger sitting on 22's they both knew it was Tiffany. When they reached the whip Rico hopped out and gave them both pounds.

"Yo let me holla at you for a second" Rico said as him and J-Murder walked to the side. When the two men walked to the side Trina headed across the street to the bodega (store).

"Yo you going to the store?"Tiffany yelled stepping out the whip.

"Yeah" Trina replied.

"Wait up I'm gonna go with you, girl those boots are cute" Tiffany said as the two disappeared into the store.

"What happened?" J-Murder asked.

"Them fucking pigs came and got me talking about Smoke got merked, them clowns was asking me a whole lot of questions and shit"

"So is Smoke dead or not?"

"I don't know, I called him and it went straight to his machine" Rico said. "But yo I gotta go to the crib and take care of something so I'ma get up with you later"

"Aight bet hit me up later cuz I need to talk to you about that nigga Buck" J-Murder said giving Rico a pound.

"Why what's up witargat nigga Buck he fucking up already?" Rico asked.

"Nah he locked that spot in the Bronx down already, I sent dat nigga Gunner over there to make sure everything goes how it's suppose to"

"Good that's what I like to hear, I'ma take care of this business then I'ma get up wit you later". Rico gave Trina a kiss on the cheek hopped in the whip and headed home.

***

Dred sat soaking in the Jacuzzi with some stripper bitch when he was interrupted by his cell phone ringing. "Yo what's the deal?"

"What's going on cuz?" Cali asked.

"Cali my nigga what's poppin?"

"I'm chilling I called to see what's up with that business"

"Oh yeah don't worry I'ma take care of that tomorrow" Dred said suddenly remembering.

"Hurry up man I did my part now you do your part" Cali's voice was calm, but strong at the same time.

"Calm down I just told you I'm gonna take care of that tomorrow"

"My bad I'm just ready to start setting shit up" Cali said. "Just holla at me when you take care of That"

***

Rico sat in the crib watching "Paid In Full" puffing on some haze. Before Rico could finish the L he felt his cell phone vibrating. When he answered the phone he heard a woman on the other end crying. "Hello"

"Hello can I speak to Rico please?" the woman sobbed into the receiver.

"Thisis Rico who's calling?"

"This is Jessica Smoke's wife"

"Hey Jessica how are you holding up?"

"I'm doing ok, Smoke told me if I needed anything to call you" she cried.

"Okay so how can I help you?" Rico asked willing to help anyway he could.

"Rico I need to talk to you but I can't do it over the phone"

"Aight let me know where your at and I'll come through and holla at you" he said pulling out a paper, and pen.

"I'll meet you at the gas station on Gun Hill Road" Jessica said.

Rico threw on some sweatpants, and a hoodie grabbed, his Beretta and Tiffany's car keys. "Yo I'll be back and I'm taking your car" Rico yelled as he walked out the door. When Jessica spotted the Charger she walked to the car and hopped in the passenger seat.

"Thank you for meeting on such short notice" she said wiping her eyes.

"Don't worry about it Ma it's nothing I'm just here to help you, are you hungry?" he asked.

"A little bit" As the two sat down to eat their food Rico noticed Jessica was still crying.

"I miss my husband" she said breaking down in tears. "I know that mufucka Dred had something to do with my Baby getting killed".

"Hold up what makes you think that?" Rico asked stuffing fries in his mouth.

"Me and Smoke had just got back from vacation but while we were gone Smoke gave me ya number and said if anything ever happened to him to call you. It sounded kind of strange so I asked him if everything was alright and he told me Dred had been acting very strange lately and how when Dred's phone rings he takes his calls outside Or something like that, but Rico he told me not to worry because he was not a 100% sure if Dred was on some funny shit or not so I really didn't pay it that much attention. Either it's me or it's a coincidence that right after Smoke puts me on about Dred he so happens to get murdered and on top of that Dred's the only mufucka who knew we was going on vacation so I figured he set Smoke up what do you think?" Jessica asked taking a bite out of her Whopper.

"Yo the shit kind of makes sense, when they wet Smoke up he was in front of ya'lls crib?"

"Yeah we had just got back from our vacation" Jessica wiped her eyes.

"Yeah something is definitely funny cuz Smoke told me the only two people who knew where ya'll lived was me and Dred" Rico remembered.

"Rico I know that mufucka had something to do wit Smoke getting killed I can feel it" Jessica said looking Rico dead in his eyes.

"Aight this is what I'm gonna do. I'm gonna do some looking into this and if I find out something else, I'll let you know and Jessica you got my word if I find out Dred had something to do wit Smoke getting merked I'll personally take care of it myself for you" he promised.

"Thank you Rico I really appreciate it"

"Don't mention it, now let's get home"

"Nah I ain't going back to dat house. I've been staying in a hotel until I find a new crib" Jessica said with a scared look on her face

"Cool you need any money?"

"Nah I'm good Smoke left me enough cake to hold me down"

Rico dropped Jessica off at the Budget hotel downtown. He then called his crew and set up a meeting at the stash crib in the Bronx so him and his crew could discuss what's been going on.

When Rico pulled up in front of the stash crib he saw Buck walking towards the building. "Yo hold up" Rico yelled as he caught up with Buck.

"What's good my nigga?" Buck said giving Rico a pound.

"Ain't nothing we got a little fuckin problem but it ain't nothing we can't fix let's get upstairs and see if everybody else is here already"

When Rico and Buck got upstairs they were happy to see the whole crew was there.

"What's going on everybody, I'm gonna make this meeting short and sweet cause I know ya'll got shit to do so let me start off by saying ya'll doing yall thing in the streets cause that paper is coming in like crazy, and Buck you stepped up ya game crazy quick. It's great to have you on the team. Now the reason I called you down here is because we might have to get rid of somebody in the family" Rico announced.

"Who you talking about?" Trina asked looking around the room.

"I'm not sure but I think we are gonna have to get rid of Dred"

J-Murder stood up and passed Buck the blunt. "What's up wit dat nigga Dred, what makes you think he's gonna be a problem?"

"I talked to Smoke's wife and she was telling me that before Smoke got killed he was telling her that Dred was acting mad funny and shit so I don't know what's good yet thats why I said we might have to get rid of him. Basically all I'm saying is to be on point it might have to go down thats it this meeting is over. I gotta get back home before Tiffany kills me" Rico said as he gave the whole crew pounds and broke out.

As Rico back up out of his parking spot he felt his cell phone vibrating. Rico looked at the caller ID and saw that it was Dred. "Yo what's Rico poppin?"

"Chillin, I'm about to call it a night and head back to the crib, why what's poppin?" Rico asked.

"Yo I need you to do me a favor and pick up 7 bricks for me tomorrow" Dred said.

"Why can't you do it?" Rico asked suspiciously.

"I gotta go to Pittsburgh in the morning and handle a few things. I got the money right here I just need you to pick it up and meet up with my new Jamaican connect"

"Jamaican connect what happen with Papi?"

"Popi is cool but the Jamaicans prices are cheaper"

"I just seen Papi the other day and we already straight for the month, what you need 7 joints for?" Rico questioned.

"It's for my man, I'm gonna over charge the nigga you already know how I get down" Dred lied.

"I don't know about them Jamaican niggaz?" Rico said skeptically.

"Don't worry about it I already told them you were coming and everything is gonna be fine. Rico I really need you to do dis favor for me"

"I'm on my way to ya crib I'll holla at you when I get there"

When Rico arrived at Dred's crib he took a seat on the couch.

"What's good you want a drink?"

"Henny" Rico replied.

"Yeah Rico I know this is some unexpected shit but I need you to hold me down, I'll be gone for 3 weeks" Dred said handing Rico his drink.

"I got you just make sure them dredlock mufuckas know I'm coming"

"Don't worry about it everything is already set up here is the buy money" Dred said handing Rico the duffle bag.

"What happen, I thought we were supposed to take care of dis Hollywood nigga a few months ago?"

"Yo I thought I told you that nigga got bodied a few months ago"

"Nah you ain't tell me, oh my fault I could have sworn I told you"

"It's all good let me get up outta here and get back to the crib" Rico said downing his drink.

The next day Rico laid in Kim's crib getting a nice oil massage thinking about what he was getting ready to do.

"Baby what's on ya mind?" Kim asked.

"Business the usual you know I stay busy".

"Yeah I know you stay busy but I don't like when you think so hard, come here let me take ya mind off that business, plus you need a clear head when you handling business" Kim said as she turned Rico on his back and placed his whole love stick in her mouth. Kim sucked on Rico's dick like a new born baby sucks on a bottle until Rico filled her mouth with his fluids. Once Rico exploded in Kim's mouth she greedily swallowed it all up and continued to suck him off until he got hard again and bust in her mouth again.

"How do you feel now?" Kim asked wiping the juices off her mouth.

"I feel much better now" Rico said with a big kool aid smile on his face. "Good looking Ma, I needed that now I gotta go take care of business"

"I hope that head and massage made you feel better baby" Kim said helping Rico put his clothes on.

"Yeah Ma I feel much better now" Rico replied kissing her on the cheek.

* * *

Trina parked the hooptie in front of the building that Rico pointed out. "Yo you sure this the building" Trina asked looking at the abandoned building.

"Yeah this the address that Dred gave me"

"Ya'll be careful cause I don't trust that nigga Dred , I think we should merk that nigga now and get it over wit" Trina said checking the magazine on her 9mm.

"I know what you saying, something just don't feel right" Rico said cocking his four fifth.

"So what you gonna do Rico it's ya call?" Gunner asked from the back seat.

"Fuck it we just gonna do this last deal until we get to the bottom of this" Rico said as him and Gunner hopped out the hooptie. " Me and Gunner gonna go in here and take care of this business real quick just make sure you keep the car running just in case cause you know how these Jamaican niggas get down". Rico grabbed the duffle bag winked at Trina and walked in the abandon building with

Gunner right by his side. Rico opened the door to the building when he stepped inside he saw the lights were very dim.

"Be on point" Rico said pulling out his four fifth. Rico and Gunner made their way up the steps with their guns drawn. When they made it to the top of the stairs they were met by three Jamaican niggaz.

"Whoa, Whoa we just here just here to do business" one of the Jamaicans said with a strong accent.

"My bad" Rico said putting his .45 in his waistband.

"So what's up, you got the money?" The Jamaican asked with a grimy look in his eyes.

"Yeah I got the money, you got the sh....."

Before Rico could even finish his sentence one of the Jamaicans pulled out a .40 caliber and popped him in the shoulder. The impact from the shot made Rico spin around causing him to drop the duffle bag. Once Rico spun around he reached for his .45 but before he could pull it out two shots to the stomach sent him flying down the stairs. When Gunner saw Rico take the first shot to the shoulder he quickly pulled out his Beretta and put a bullet in one of the Jamaicans dredlocks. Before the other Jamaican could react Gunner put four in his chest sending the man crashing through the wooden door. When Gunner turned around to pop the last Jamaican he found himself staring down the barrel of .357 The last Jamaican pulled the trigger and left Gunner's brains on the wall.

When Trina heard the shots she hopped out the hooptie and headed towards the abandon building. Trina stepped inside the building and saw Rico at the bottom of the stairs leaking. As Trina got closer to Rico's body she heard footsteps coming from upstairs. Trina bent down to check Rico's pulse and was startled when she heard him whisper "Yo T that mufucka upstairs shot me, yo handle that nigga". Trina tip toed her way up the stairs. When she made it to the top she saw Gunner laid out on the floor with his brains next to him. "Damn Gunner" she said to herself as she turned the corner. When Trina turned the corner she saw a man with dredlocks looking in Rico's duffle bag.

"Hey rude boy" she called out. When the Jamaican turned around Trina emptied the whole clip into his chest killing him instantly. Trina made it back downstairs with Rico's duffle bag around her neck and saw that Rico had passed out from to much blood loss. She immediately dragged Rico outside. It took everything Trina had to get Rico in the backseat but she got it done. Once Rico was in the car Trina jumped behind the wheel and headed to the hospital doing 90 miles per hour. "Hang in there Rico I got you" Trina said out loud while weaving in and out of traffic. Trina pulled in front of the hospital beeping the horn like a mad woman. "somebody help me" she yelled stepping out of the car. Seconds later several doctors came running towards the car. They placed Rico on a stretcher and rushed him into the hospital. As

Trina stood there watching a cracker wearing a doctor's outfit approached her.

"Excuse me Ma'm do you know what happened to that gentleman, were you with him when he got shot?" he asked.

"Nah I found him like that" Trina said walking off.

"Ms. I'm not finished talking to you, hey somebody stop that lady!" The man screamed. Trina ran to the hooptie and stepped on the gas leaving the smell of burnt rubber in the air.

CHAPTER TEN

Tiffany sat in the tub relaxing and enjoying her bubble bath listening to the sounds of Mary J. Blige. She had just got back from shopping, while she was out she picked up some sexy lingerie from Victoria Secret and planned on modeling for Rico when he got home. Tiffany sat singing with Mary when she heard the house phone ringing. She grabbed the phone off the hamper and answered it. "Hello"

"Tiff this is Trina"

"Hey wassup?" Tiffany asked wondering why Trina was calling the house.

"Rico just got shot!"

"Oh my God where is he?"

"I dropped him off at Harlem Hospital" Trina answered.

"Is he okay?"

"I'm not going to lie to you, I don't know"

Married To Da Streets

Tiffsaid hung up the phone, hopped out the tub dried, off threw on some sweatpants, a tee shirt and some Jordan's. She threw her hair in a ponytail and flew out the door. When Tiffany made it to the hospital she was told that she couldn't see Rico so she sat in the waiting area until she heard something. The next morning the doctor woke Tiffany up.

"Ma'm are you here for Rico Anderson?"

"Yes is he alright?" Tiffany asked nervously.

"Yes he's going to be fine, Ma'm what is your name?"

"Tiffany, why?"

"Cause he asked me to come get you" The doctor said.

"How did he know I was here?" she wondered. The doctor escorted Tiffany to Rico's room, when she saw Rico laying in the hospital bed she broke down into tears. "Hey Daddy, you alright?" Tiffany asked as she kissed Rico on the forehead.

"Stop crying Baby I'm alright"

"What happened Baby?" Tiffany asked.

"I got caught slippin, don't worry Baby everything gonna be alright" Rico told her.

"Babyl was worried, I was so scared I was gonna lose you" Tiffany sat in the hospital for seven days with Rico until he was released. Tiffany did everything for Rico until he recovered.

***

Rico sat on the couch watching the Lakers beat the shit out the Knicks when Tiffany came and handed him a plate.

"Baby I think it's time for us to get a bigger crib" Tiffany said.

"Alright start looking for a crib you like and we gonna make it happen" He said as if it was nothing. Tiffany took Rico's plate sat it on the coffee table and got on her knees.

"What are you doing Baby?"

"Shh I got dis" Tiffany said placing her warm lips on Rico's dick. Rico sat back and watched his wife's mouth slide off and on his dick. Tiffany then got up took off her shirt, slid her thong to the side and climbed on Rico and started bouncing viciously on his dick. "Uhm ride dis dick" Rico moaned as he gripped both of Tiffany's ass cheeks. Tiffany continued to ride her man. Rico and Tiffany both came together and just laid on the couch holding each other. Rico was about to doze off until he heard the house phone ringing. "Baby grab that phone off the coffee table". "Hello?"

"What's good my Nigga?" J-Murder said on the other line.

"You tell me you ain't been out the crib since you came home"

"Me and Buck on our way over to come get you out the house"J-Murder said.

"Aight I'll be waiting B. One"

J-Murder pulled up in front of Rico's crib in a new 2009 black Impala sitting on 20's. "Where the fuck is dis nigga at?" J-Murder said beeping the horn. Two minutes later Rico came walking out his crib shining.

"Damn nigga is ya jewelry bright enough?" Buck said playfully.

"Come on son you know I only rock ice that glows in the dark" Rico said hopping in the backseat. "So what's up where ya'll wanna go?"

J-Murder smiled. "I got the perfect place"

J-Murder jumped on the highway pumping J ay Z. J-Murder pulled up in the strip club parking lot. "Aight let's go in here have a good time and talk some business"

"Oh yeah before we go inside did you bring that for me?" Rico asked.

"Oh shit yeah I got dat in the trunk" J-Murder said popping the trunk, when he returned he handed Rico a bullet proof vest.

"Niggas ain't gonna catch me slippin again" Rico said putting his white tee over the vest and giving Buck a pound. The three men entered the club and made their way to a small section in the corner.

"So what's up wit them niggaz that popped you?" J-Murder asked.

"That nigga Dred had me set up"

"Get the fuck outta here you bullshitting" J-Murder said in disbelief.

"Nah I'm dead ass"
"Why you ain't tell us we could have taken care of thatt nigga" J-Murder said sipping on his Henny.

"Be easy I had to let a little time pass so the jakes don't be on my ass. Dat faggot ass Det. Ford came up to the hospital asking me a thousand questions talking about as soon as I slip up his gonna be there to lock me up" Rico said.

"So what's up wit that nigga Dred?" J-Murder asked taking another sip of his Henny.

"We gonna take care of that nigga in two days, that clown said he was gonna be outta town but I know dat mufucka is still in New York. He's probably still at his crib but thats what I want cause I'm gonna rock him to sleep" Rico said. As the two men continued their conversation J-Murder spotted a dark skin thick chick grillin him. "Yeah but like I was saying when we get at this nigga Dred we taking everything from the nigga. Money, weight, jewelry, cars everything" J-Murder said giving Rico a pound.

"I'ma bring one of my homies just in case shit gets a little ugly" Buck said flashing his gold teeth. J-Murder stood up and finished his drink. "Come here baby" he called out to the stripper.

The dark skin chick had been grilling J-Murder she approached their table looking like a model. She walked up to the table wearing a lime green thong with matching top along with a pair of stilettos. "You talking to me?" The woman asked standing directly in front of J-Murder.

"Yeah I'm talking to you I seen you over there grillin me so I wanted to see what's good" J-Murder said grinning. The woman could tell that J-Murder was getting money by the jewelry that he and his friends wore.

"I was only looking at you cause you was looking at me" the stripper said seductively.

"Aight Ma come and have a drink wit me" When the girl bent down to have a seat J-Murder's eyes were locked on her fatty. "So Ma what's ya name?"

"Everybody calls me Sparkle" she said sipping on some Henny.

"So what do people call you?" Sparkle asked.

"Everybody calls me J-Murder"

J-Murder and Sparkle sat talking until the club closed. Rico and Buck had both hopped in cabs and went home for a few hours. Later that night J-Murder dropped Sparkle off at her crib and spent the night.

The next day Rico planned on going to see his mother. Trina had called and told Rico that his mother was doing real good so he was gonna pay her a visit. Rico dicked Tiffany down put her to sleep hopped in the shower got dressed and broke out. When Rico walked toward the building he saw Trina and Wolverine chilling on the bench. "What's poppin?" Rico said giving them both pounds.

"Out here grindin B but fuck all that, what's good wit them fools that tried to end ya career?" Wolverine asked.

"It ain't nothing me and J-Murder gonna make that happen tomorrow" Rico said taking the blunt from Wolverine. "What's up with you and Trina, why you sittin over there all quiet?"

"I'm over here stressed out" Trina exhaled.

"Why what's up?" Rico asked.

"I gotta go to jail next week, my court day is in 4 days" Trina huffed.

"Damn I forgot all about that shit don't worry abtabletat shit Ma you gonna be alright that 8 months is gonna fly past"

"Yeah I know but it's just about the point of being there. I know I'ma be fine I just ain't to excited to be around a whole bunch of bum ass bitches all day for 8 months" Trina vented.

"Don't worry you gonna be alright, come upstairs wit me so I can holla at my Moms"

Rico and Trina hopped off the pissy elevator and headed down the hallway. Rico opened the door with his key and saw an empty house. "Damn where my Mom's at?"

"She probably at work" Trina said as they left the crib.

"I'm about to get up outta here, you stay strong aight" Rico said kissing Trina on the cheek.

"I'm cool you just make sure you get home safe and tell Tiffany I said what's up" Trina said as she watched Rico pull off. When Rico broke out Trina went and copped some trees from Goggles hopped in her Lexus and headed to the liquor store. When she got in her crib she took her clothes off and got fucked up until she fell asleep.

***

Rico threw his vest on over his long john shirt, threw on his black gloves, grabbed his four fifth and walked out the crib. When Rico stepped out his crib he saw J-Murder, Buck and some other guy standing in front of a Ford Explorer wearing all black.

"What's good?" Rico said giving J-Murder and Buck a pound.

"Nigga you ready to get it poppin?" Buck asked pulling his dreds in a ponytail. "Oh yeah this my man right here I been telling you about Bull, yo Bull this Rico" he introduced the two.

Bull was 6'3'' and weighed 235 pounds. He had black jeans, black gloves, and a black hoodie. Bull's face had a ice grill looking like he had a license to kill.

"Come on let's go make this nigga a memory" J-Murder said as he got behind the steering wheel and pulled off. J-Murder parked the Explorer a block away from Dred's crib.

"Listen we gonna go in there peel these niggas caps back and be the fuck out. I don't give a fuck who ya'll shoot just don't shoot that clown ass nigga cuz he's mines" Rico said loading his four fifth. Bull loaded his 12 gauge shotgun, Buck loaded his Uzi and J-Murder cocked his two berettas. Once everybody got their shit together the 4 men crept to the side of Dred's front door. On the count of three Bull kicked in the door.

Dred sat in the crib with a flew of his flunkies and a few young ladies. Everybody was drinking and enjoying themselves listening to 50 Cent's new CD. Dred sat on the couch with a beautiful young lady on his lap, when he heard the door fly open and saw J-Murder, Bull, and Buck standing in his doorway he damn near shitted on himself.

"What the fuck are ya'll doing here?" Dred asked looking confused.

"You know what the fuck we doing here?" Rico said walking through the front door.

"Hey Rico what's all this about?" Dred asked in a shaky voice.

"You know exactly what this is all about you fuckin snake, yo Buck let them niggas have it" Rico orderd. PAT TAT TAT TAT BOOM BOOM BOOM Buck and Bull killed everybody in the crib even the females. The only person they didn't shoot was Dred.

"Wait a minute Rico you don't have to do this, I don't even know what's going on"

"Mufucka you was supposed to be in Pittsburgh!" Rico growled.

"Um Um..."

"Shut the fuck up" Rico said cutting him off. "Listen just tell me why you set me up and why you got Smoke killed"

Rico I swear I would never...."

"Stop fuckin lying "Rico said as he shot Dred in the leg.

"Okay wait I'll tell you everything, I was jealous cause Smoke put you on. Not just cuz he put you on but I was jealous of how you blew up so fast and once you blew up Smoke started brushing me off and I wasn't feeling that. Then this mufucka from L.A. named Cali gave me an offer I couldn't refuse so I set the whole thang up"

"Aight who is this Cali mufucka that I keep hearing about?" Rico asked.

"He's some wild nigga from Compton with a bunch of killers that will do anything he says" Dred said.

"Okay where can I find this clown at?"

"Rico please you ain't gonna do nothing but start a war"

"You sound like a fuckin pussy tell me where the fuck we can find these clowns at" Rico spat.

"Rico Cali never tells me where he rests his head, the only time I see him is when he calls me or I call him and we meet up"

"So you telling me you don't know where this nigga Cali is at right?" Rico huffed. "Gimme his number" Rico said pulling out his cell phone. Rico stored Cali's number in his cell phone and decided not to call him. "Listen Dred I want all ya money and you already know I want all the coke so please let's make this as easy as possible"

"I got about $50,000 upstairs and the rest of my money is in my other apartment in Queens along wit the bricks"

"Gimme the address" Rico said. Once Dred wrote down the address Rico handed the piece of paper to J-Murder. "You, Buck, and Bull go get that paper".

"Rico you can have anything you want please just don't kill me" Dred begged sounding like a bitch.

"I'm sorry but I can't do That" Rico said aiming his four fifth at Dred's face. Rico emptied his whole clip in Dred's face. Rico then went upstairs and threw the $50 gees in a book bag, grabbed all of Dred's jewelry put a new clip in his .45 and walked out the front door.

Rico hopped in Dred's Benz stashed the heat under the seat and pulled off. When he got home, he saw Tiffany still in her bra and panties. "Baby hurry up and dress warm because it's chilly outside" Rico said as he went in the bedroom to change. When Tiffany finally finished getting dressed she had on some high heel gator boots, some black jeans and a thin black leather jacket. Her hair was neatly pulled back in a ponytail and her lips were shining from Cherry lip gloss. Rico came out the bedroom wearing all black with a red

Pelle leather jacket and a red Cincinnati Reds fitted cap. When they finally made it outside Tiffany was on him.

"Where did you get this car from?"

"You like it?"

"Hell yeah I like it"

"What you wanna eat tonight?" Rico asked quickly changing the subject.

"I been craving for some spaghetti all day"

Rico pulled up in front of the Italian restaurant he grabbed the heat from under the seat and tucked it in his waistband. "Come on Baby I'm hungrier then a mufucka". After dinner Rico and Tiffany just sat and enjoyed each others company. "Baby I got some good news and I got a surprise for you" Tiffany said taking a bite of dessert. "Which one you want first?"

"Oh boy here we go, I need some good news right about now so why don't you hit me with the good news first"

"Well first of all I've been looking around like you told me to and I found us a nice house Baby and guess what?"

"What?"

"It only cost $300,000 and its right there on the lower East Side" Tiffany said.

"Okay now what's the surprise?"

"Okay you want me to just come out and say it?" Tiffany asked.

"Yeah"

"Rico I'm pregnant!" She said excitedly.

"Pregnant?"

"Yes I've been waiting to tell you, damn what you not happy?" Tiffany noticing the disappointment on his face.

"Of course i am, I just hope it's a boy"

"You crazy my first one is going to be a girl" Tiffany said smiling from ear to ear. Rico and Tiffany got back in the Benz and Rico stashed the heat under the seat. "Yo you need to get a stash box in all of our cars cause we can't afford for you to be getting locked up over no dumb shit" said Tiffany.

"Listen Ma let me handsaifyis I already smileyat taken care of" Rico said blasting Jay Z's Hard knock Life Vol. 2.

***

In Cali's office stood Hulk, Youngin, and a few soldiers. Cali was heated he didn't like how Rico had killed Dred and fucked up his plans. Now the streets were watching and Cali had to do something. The only thing left for him to do was to pop something. "Yo Hulk you heard anything about them niggas?"

"Yeah my man told me them niggas is throwing a party at a Club Exit"

"Round up the goons to pay them niggas a visit tonight" Cali said taking a long drag on the blunt.

* * *

When Rico and Tiffany pulled up in the hood it seemed like the whole projects was outside ready to go to Trina's going away party. Everyone was dressed to impress. Rico had given everybody the night off. The only people who stayed behind were the soldiers who were too young to party. So instead of partying they spent the night getting money. Seconds later Buck and Bull pulled up in Buck's Malibu. Buck stepped out the whip carrying a bottle of Moet in each hand.

"Damn it's a lot of people showing Trina love tonight" Tiffany said looking shocked at how many people were in front of one building.

"When you show love you get love" Rico said.

"Well I'm gonna show you a whole bunch of love when we get home Daddy" Tiffany said with a sexy look on her face. When Trina finally made it downstairs she looked like a million bucks. She had on some all white high heel Fendi boots, some white skin tight stretch pants, a white halter top and to top it off she wore an all white mink. She had her hanging down from a fresh dubie killing it.

When everybody finally made it to the club the shit was jumping it was so crowded a mufucka could barely move. Rico and his crew maxed out in their VIP section chilling and drinking getting bodied. Trina was on the dance floor doing her thing with a bottle of Moet in her hand. Rico and Tiffany hit the dance floor also dancing to the sounds of 50 Cent's "Candy Shop". J-Murder sat in VIP with Sparkle sitting on his lap while he and Wolverine had some words. Everything was going smooth until Tiffany saw Peaches all up in Rico's face.

"Why is that bitch all up in his face like that" Tiffany said to herself as she approached them. "Excuse me Baby why is this bitch all up in ya mouth?"

"Bitch, who you calling a bitch?" Peaches said throwing her hair in a ponytail.

"Bitch you the only bitch I see all up in my man's face, what's really good?" Tiffany said not backing down.

Before Peaches could say another word Rico gave her a look like bitch that's enough.

"Oh I'm sorry I didn't know you was his girl, I ain't mean to step on ya toes Ma" Peaches said giving Rico a look that said call me later as she walked off.

"Whatever bitch" Tiffany said focusing all her attention on Rico. "What's up wit that, how you gonna have a bitch all up in ya face while I'm here?"

"What you talking about, you didn't even give me a chance to tell the bitch I had a girl" Rico said.

"Rico stop playing wit me cause you gonna make me fuck somebody up" Tiffany said as the two made their way back to the couch in their VIP booth. At around 2am Cali and Hulk walked up in the club shining with about 16 soldiers behind them. Cali and his crew went straight to the bar then to their VIP booth. As soon as Cali and his blood niggas sat down hoes were piling up in their booth trying to be down with the niggas getting money. Within 10 minutes Cali was getting head from some shorty with the crazy fat ass. He bust off in her mouth and dismissed her. Cali hated gold diggers the only bitch he would ever give money to was his wife Simone all the other bitches he just used and abused. Tiffany sat back in the VIP booth with Rico just having a good time.

"Baby I'll be right back, I got to run to the ladies room real quick". As Tiffany made her way through the crowded club she felt somebody grab her wrist. When she looked up she saw that it was Rick her ex boyfriend. "What you doing here Rick?" Tiffany asked snatching her hand away.

"Damn Tiff you looking good, what's really good?"

"What's really good, nothing, Rick I ain't seen you in 4 years I know you don't think your just gonna come back and snatch me up" Tiffany rolled her eyes.

"Nah Ma it's not even like dat I'm out in Cali getting this money now. The reason why I bounced was because I couldn't do anything for you but now it's different as you can see, now I'm getting paper" Rick said popping the collar on his mink.

"Listen Rick you buggin I already got a man" Tiffany said as she went to the restroom. When Tiffany came out the restroom Rick was right there waiting for her.

"Come on Baby let me buy you a drink"

"Nah I'm good why don't you buy some other girl a drink, excuse me I gotta get back cause my man is waiting for me"

"Fuck ya man" Rick said jumping into Tiffany's path. "I'm not letting you get away from me this time the last time...." As Rick was talking he felt the cold steel on the back of his head.

"What's up Baby, who is this clown?"Rico asked Tiffany.

"This is Rick my old boyfriend"

"So what's up you was over here reminiscing?" Rico asked with a hint of jealously.

"Rico don't even play yourself I was trying to get back to our booth but he wouldn't let me leave" Tiffany told him.

"Aight Baby go back over to our booth and finish enjoying yourself" Rico said. Tiffany kissed Rico's lips and went back to the booth. "Aight fams what's really good wit you?"

"I don't know who you are but your making a big mistake, I fucks wit Cali and when he finds out what ya doing it's gonna be trouble for you" Rick huffed.

"Does it look like I give a fuck about a Cali, nigga fuck you and Cali. Matter of fact take this shit off" Rico said taking all of Rick's jewelry. "Take that bullshit mink off too, matter of fact get butt naked". When Rick finally got butt naked Rico cracked him in the head twice with the burner leaving Rick's head leaking. "Now go tell ya boss I said suck my dick".

When Rico got back to his booth he was all over Tiffany. "Yo why you had that nigga all up in ya face?"

"Rico he wouldn't leave me alone, Rico you are too jealous you know I'm all yours and I ain't going no anywhere"

"Next time don't be having no bum ass nigga in ya face" Rico barked.

"Okay baby it won't happen again" Tiffany said kissing Rico.

Cali and his crew searched the club looking for Rico he really crossed the line when he did what he did to Rick. As Hulk squeezed through the crowded club looking for Rico he spotted some chick looking real good in her white outfit. "Damn Shorty got the bubble" Hulk said to himself. "thats definitely wife material" he thought as he approached her. "What's good Ma?"

"Ain't shit" Trina responded drunk as hell.

"I been watching you all night and I was wondering if I could take you to get something to eat sometime" Hulk offered.

"Nigga please" Trina said laughing in his face.

"What's so funny?"

"Yothruats what's funny" Trina capped back.

"Stop frontin Ma you know you wanna suck my dick". When Hulk said dat Trina flipped out.

"What the fuck you just said?"

"Bitch you heard me" He repeated himself. SPLASH.

When Hulk called Trina a bitch she threw her drink in his face. When Hulk felt the liquid on his face, he quickly stole on Trina knocking her out with one punch. J -Murder was on the floor dancing with Sparkle when he saw Trina throw a drink in some big guy's face. By the time J-Murder got to where Trina was at she was already laid out. J-Murder immediately two pieced Hulk sending the big man stumbling backwards. Once Hulk regained his balance he and J-Murder got they thump on. When Rico saw everybody on the dance floor shift to one side he stood up and saw J-Murder getting it on with some big nigga. When Rico looked to his left he saw Rick walking through the club butt naked with something chrome in his hand. Rico quickly pulled out the burner and hit Rick four times in the chest killing him on the spot. When the shots went off the whole club got low and started stampeding to get out the club. When Hulk heard the gunshots he pushed J-Murder off of him and pulled out his Desert Eagle. J-Murder saw the Desert Eagle and quickly grabbed some girl who was desperately trying to get out the club and used her as a shield. BOOM BOOM BOOM BOOM the bullets from the Desert Eagle tore the woman apart. J-Murder threw the girl on the floor and ran towards the exit. As he was running he pulled out his four fifth and threw a few shots over his shoulder not caring who he hit. When Trina woke up she saw everybody running and screaming trying to get out the club. She immediately grabbed her handbag off the wet floor and pulled out her .380. Trina got up and saw 4 men with guns trying to creep up on Buck from the behind. She quickly cocked the heat back and let all 4 of the gunmen have it. Rico held Tiffany's wrist as the two ran for the exit. When Cali saw Rico and Tiffany trying to get up out the club he pulled out his two Berettas and opened fire on the couple. Bullets flew past Rico and Tiffany's head as they ran towards the exit pushing and stepping over people in the process. When Rico and Tiffany made it to Rico's truck they didn't notice Youngin creeping on them from behind. Before Youngin could pull the trigger 6 shots sent him to the pavement. When Rico turned around he saw Wolverine standing over Youngin with his 9mm smoking. "I owe you one" Rico said as him, Wolverine, and Tiffany hopped in the Escalade and pulled off.

***

The next morning Rico and the whole crew stood in the courtroom showing Trina support as the judge remanded her and sentenced her to 8 months at Rose M. Singer Correctional Facility. Trina took her time like a G when the court officer cuffed her and took her to the back. " Yo I gotta go see that nigga Det. Lance real quick as soon as I get back we gonna have a meeting so make sure everybody is at the spot in about an hour" Rico said giving J Murder a pound before he walked out the courtroom.

CHAPTER ELEVEN

Det. Ford stood parked across the street from the projects watching the fiends come and go. "Yeah get all that crack money while you can, cause I'm about to shut this shit down" he said to himself.

As Det. Ford staked out the projects he saw Pooky coming out of the building. "Yeah I got ya ass now" Det. Ford said as he threw on his hoodie and stepped out of the car. Pooky was so thirsty to take a blast he didn't notice Ford running up from behind him. "Don't move shit head" Ford yelled as he stuck his .357 in Pooky's back.

"Yo what the..."

"Shut the fuck up before I put you in a fucking wheelchair" Ford said as he threw Pooky in the backseat of his car. "Listen up because I'm only gonna say this once, what floor is Rico's operation on?"

"Uhm he switches floors everyday" Pooky stuttered.

"Motherfucker what floor are they on tonight?" Ford asked pressing his .357 to Pooky's temple.

"Goggles is on the eighth floor in staircase B"

"What he working with up there?" Ford asked.

"He got the crack in the other building, some other guy got the dog food"

"Pooky you know if I take you in you gonna do some real jbalance right?" Ford threatened.

"Yeah I know man give me a break, I ain't hurt nobody" Pooky pleaded.

"Aight I tell you what I'm gonna do, I'm gonna let you run the streets and do what you wanna do"

"And what's in it for you?" Pooky asked.

"All you gotta do is keep me posted on what's going on in the projects and in return I'll keep you out of jail" Ford offered.

"Damn I don't know Rico is my man I don't know if I could cross him"

"Listen either you work for me or you go to jail, what's it gonna be?"

***

Rico and Kim sat in Madison Square Garden along with J-Murder and Sparkle watching the Knicks take on the Lakers. "Damn this nigga Kobe is busting the Knicks ass" Rico said giving J-Murder a pound. After the game the two couples made there way to BBQ's. As the four sat enjoying their food two men approached them wearing hoodies.

"Excuse me I don't mean to interrupt but ya name is Rico right?" one of the men asked.

"Who wants to know?" Rico asked aiming his four fifth at the man's dick under the table.

"Nah it's not even like that "said the hoodied man. " They call me Rocks andaThs is my man Sticks we been trying to get up wit you for the longest. We heard you got that butta (good coke) you think I could get ya number so we can do some business?"

"Yo homeboy check this out me and my man is chillin with our shorties right now. I don't know nothing about what you talking about right now smell me?"

"Come on what you think we cops are something?" Sticks asked.

"Yo my man it's a time and place for everything and now is not the time or place, now if yall will excuse me I'm tryin to have dinner wit my shorty right now" Rico said in an aggravated tone.

"Aight Rico I'ma let you finish doing ya thang. Here's my number holla at me when you ready to do some business" Rocks said as he handed Rico a piece of paper. Rocks and Sticks then made their exit.

"Yo J you ever seen them before?" Rico asked.

"Nah If you ask me I think their either the Feds are stick up kids" J-Murder answered.

"Them clowns just fucked my whole night up" Rico said placing his .45 back in his waistband.

"Baby don't even worry about them broke ass niggas you already know how niggas start hating when they see somebody doing better then them" Kim said rubbing Rico's neck. After dinner the two couples went their separate ways.

***

Tiffany loved her new house. It had 4 bedrooms and 3 bathrooms. For the last week she spent all her time decorating the new house. Rico had been spending a lot of time in the house since Tiffany was pregnant. He wanted to make sure she felt comfortable in their new house. Rico had hooked up the basement for himself. He put a big screen TV down there along with a pool table so when his niggas came over they didn't have to play in the living room. Rico and Tiffany loved their new house and they made sure they had sex in every part of the house. After dinner Rico went upstairs to watch Showtime at the Apollo but when he stepped into the bedroom and saw Tiffany laying on the bed with her red thong on he suddenly had a change of plans. Rico piped Tiffany down and put her straight to sleep.

* * *

J-Murder stood in building 5 with the rest of the crew and some other niggas from the projects rolling dice.

"What up nigga four gees in it" Marcus said shaking up the dice. Marcus was an old school nigga in his late thirty's. He used to be the man before he caught a 10 year bid. Now he was just another nigga trying to make some paper. "Yo what's up four gees in it who want it, what's up?"

"Yo stop the four" Buck said while he was talking on his cell phone.

"Aight say no more four coming out" Marcus said violently rolling the dice. "Come on let's go head cracks time to get the bread back" Marcus said throwing the dice his first roll was 1, 2, 6

"yeah mufucka you bout to go to 155th St. In a minute"some guy in the crowd yelled. On Marcus's second roll he rolled a four. "Yeah niggas you gonna either get down or lay down" Marcus said giving his peoples pounds.

Married To Da Streets

Buck pulled out a brick of money with 2 rubber bands wrapped around it, peeled off $4,000 and handed it to Marcus. "Take dis four and I got eight stopped" Buck said pulling out another brick of money. "Aight $8000 going to Buck ". " Let's go get dis money" Marcus said as he threw the dice. His first roll was a three

"Tracy" Buck said picking up the dice. "What's up I got a gee four and better" said Buck.

"I got dat" Marcus said being thirsty. Buck's first roll was 4, 5, 6 "headcracks nigga can I get paid, can I get paid?" Buck said giving J-Murder and Bull both pounds. Marcus handed Buck nine gees and pulled Buck to the side.

"Yo son that was my last money you think I could get $500 back?" he asked.

"Get the fuck out my face with that bullshit" Buck waved Marcus off.

"Yo who you think you talking to like that, nigga I'm OG up in dis bitch you better recognize mufucker" Marcus said all up in Buck's face. Buck quickly pulled out his banger and stabbed Marcus twice in the stomach sending him stumbling back to the mailbox.

***

Rico sat in his Mom's crib waiting for her to come home. "Yo fuck that I'm out" Rico said throwing his leather on. When Rico came downstairs he saw cops everywhere. "What the fuck is going on?" Rico thought to himself as he kept it moving. When he reached the middle of the projects he saw his whole crew. "Yo what the fuck is going on?"

"I had to put the hawk to that nigga Marcus" Buck said giving Rico a pound. "Over some money shit"

"Say no more" Rico said as he walked up to J-Murder. "What's good wit the workers and all that?"

"Everything is straight I just finished making rounds, making sure them niggas is straight"

"Thats what's up keep them niggas on they job" He said turning to face Buck. "Yo Buck what's good everything running smoothly in the Bronx?"

"Yeah the crack house is poppin off my niggas got everything on smash over there" Buck said answering his ringing cell phone.

After the cops left Rico and his crew noticed a white Expedition pull up on the corner blasting Destiny's Child "I Need a Soldier"

Who the fuck is that everybody wondered. When the light skin woman stepped out the truck niggas was beasting. "Damn look at Shorty she got the fatty" was all you heard.

"Ya'll niggaz be easy thats me right there" Rico said as he went to go greet Peaches.

"Damn this nigga gets all the pussy" said one of Rico's flunky's siad. When Rico made it to the Expedition Peaches was all over him.

"Hey Baby what's up" she said as she hugged and kissed Rico.

"What's up I thought we was going out tonight?" Peaches said.

"Oh shit I forgot all about that shit Ma I been mad busy"

"I can tell you look mad tired"

"Yeah I know but you looking mad good" Rico said palming Peaches's ass so everybody could see he was the man. "I promise I'm going to make this up to you"

"Just let me know when you got some free time cause I don't want to bump into ya wife no more" Peaches joked.

"Aight dis Saturday we gonna make it happen"

"Okay thats cool but I need some of dat dick right now, you got enough time to hibuilding with me?" Peaches asked giving Rico her best I wanna fuck you so bad face.

"Fuck a tele let's hit up the back seat of ya truck" he suggested.

"Rico you so nasty, Come on before I change my mind" Peaches said as she hopped behind the steering wheel and drove to a deserted block. When Peaches pulled over she whipped out Rico's dick, threw it in her mouth and sucked it like it was the last dick on earth.

"Damn Baby thats what's up" Rico moaned grabbing a hand full of Peaches hair. Rico stroked Peaches mouth until he couldn't take it any longer and finally exploded in her mouth. When Rico's dick got hard again he threw on a condom grabbed Peaches hand and led her to the front of the truck, where he hit it from behind. "Oh shit Rico yes Baby fuck me Baby" Peaches moaned as she threw the ass back at Rico. All Rico heard was Peaches pussy making loud slurping sounds as he dug her back out. "Throw dat shit back" Rico yelled as he slapped Peaches's ass repeatedly until he came again. "A yo take me to the corner store so I can get a hero" Rico said as the two hopped back in the Expo. As Peaches pulled off Rico felt his cell phone vibrating he looked at the caller ID and saw it was J-Murder. "Yo what's good"?

"This bitch Susan said she needs to talk to you about something"

The fiend Susan?" Rico asked making sure they were talking about the same person.

"Yeah"

"Aight what apartment she live in?"

"Building 5 apartment 5J"

"I'll be there in a minute" After Rico copped his sandwich Peaches dropped him off right where she picked him up from.

Wolverine sat on the bench and watched Rico and Peaches say their good byes. "This bitch ass nigga out here getting all the money and all the pussy and all I'm getting is peanuts. I'm the one out here bodying niggaz, and what I got to show for it? A Range Rover, a Condo, and a couple of hundred thousand fuck that I deserve more then that" Wolverine thought as he watched Rico walk into building 5. "This mufucka is in for a surprise if he thinks I'm gonna be his fucking flunky" Wolverine said thinking of a plan to take shit over.

When Rico stepped inside Susan's crib it was a mess. Clothes were everywhere and dishes were overflowing in the sink. As Rico stepped in the living room he saw Susan's daughter Heather sitting on the couch watching TV. From the look of Heather she had to be either 11 or 12 years old.

"What you got to talk to me about Susan. Make it fast cuz I ain't got all day" Rico in an unpleasant tone.

"Okay Rico I know I owe you $400 but I need a favor" Susan said.

"A favor?" Rico echoed. "Susan I think you all out of favors"

"Wait Rico I need $200 or they gonna try to put me and my daughter on the street" Susan said.

"How you gonna smoke up ya rent money?"

"Rico I'm trying to stop but it's hard" Susan responded.

"So you telling me you wanna quit?"

"Yes Rico I been trying to quit for the longest" she said as she broke down into tears. As Rico was talking to Susan he heard Heather's stomach growling crazy loud. "Damn that was her stomach? I know that wasn't that lil girl's stomach?" Rico said walking towards the refrigerator. When Rico opened the refrigerator it wasn't shit in it but a box of baking soda and two empty ice trays. "Yo Susan how you gonna how this little girl in this dirty ass house wit no food?"

"Rico I need help" Susan said dropping to her knees crying like a baby. Rico went in the living room and gave Heather his sandwich. "Here put that in ya stomach"

"Thank you Rico" Heather said innocently.

Married To Da Streets

"Yo Susan check this out, this what I'm gonna do for you I'm gonna give you the $200 to pay the rent and tomorrow I'm gonna get you a bed at the rehab center"

"But what about Heather, I ain't got nobody to take care of her" Susan cried.

"Aight I'm gonna take heather until you get yourself together"

"Oh thank you so much" Susan said giving Rico a big hug.

"Listen Susan you make sure you get ya shit together, I'm gonna be coming to that center to check up on you so make sure you do what you gotta do" Rico said seriously.

"What about the $400 that I owe ya peoples?" she asked.

"Listen don't worry about all that just start packing ya shit, oh yeah I'm gonna need to use this crib until you get ya self together" Rico added.

"Okay I don't have a problem wit that, let me go say bye to my baby first" Susan said as she went in the living room and explained everything to Heather.

Rico knew Tiffany was gonna flip out when he brought the little girl to the crib but his heart wouldn't let him leave the little girl for dead like that. Once Heather had her things packed her and Rico walked out the door. "Yo Susan I'm gonna come through tomorrow pay ya rent and get you in that program. You betta get ya shit together Susan cause this little girl needs you" Rico said coldly as him and Heather broke out.

* * *

Cali and Hulk sat in I HOPS thinking of a master plan on how they were gonna take shit over. "Yo my man out in Queens said everything is running smoothly out there, he said the cliental is growing everyday plus J.J already got our spot in the Bronx jumping like the playoffs" Cali said sipping his Orange juice. "Everything is taken care of all we gotta do is figure out what we gonna do wit this nigga Rico cause that mufucka needs to be taught a lesson"

"fuck that let me go handle that nigga" Hulk said looking like a maniac. "I ain't shot a nigga in a minute"

"Check dis out I want you and a few soldiers to go and push that nigga wig back, Hulk listen to me don't come back until that nigga Rico is finished" Cali said sternly.

"Listen you ain't got to tell me twice I know how to get a nigga" Hulk said giving Cali a pound. "Once you take that nigga out then we can take the nigga empire over and show these New York niggas how to really get money"

"Don't worry Rico will be finished and he's not even gonna see it coming" Hulk promised.

* * *

Tiffany and Heather got along great. Tiffany took Heather everywhere. They went shopping together, they got their hair and feet done together. Heather even got her own room filled with teddy bears and a whole bunch of other shit. Heather was loving her new life, after seeing how Rico and Tiffany lived she knew she would never be going back to how she used to live no matter what.

***

When Trina walked through those visiting room doors she had a smile from ear to ear when she saw Rico sitting waiting for her. "Hey Rico what's poppin?"

"You tell me what's poppin" Rico said kissing Trina on the cheek. "So how is it in here?"

"It's alright it's not how people think it is" Trina answered. "It's a lot of dikes in here"

"Yo you betta not be letting them bitches take advantage of you"

"Come on Rico you know I ain't with that licky licky shit plus these bitches respect my gangsta but fuck all that what's going on in the streets?"

"Same ole shit you know the game don't change just the players" Rico said holding Trina's hands. " But yo everything is good niggas is still getting This dough, you know I'm putting your paper to the side until you come home, other then that everything is cool". "Ya'll ain't bump into that nigga Cali again?"

"Nah the last time we seen him or his crew was that night at the club".

"Yo Rico don't sleep on that nigga i don't trust them niggas"

"Listen Trina let me worry about all that all I want you to worry about is these last 4 months you gotta do" Right after Rico said that this big fat CO bitch yelled "visit is over". Rico stood up and gave Trina a hug and kissed her on the cheek then headed towards the exit.

***

Wolverine walked up to his Lexus and threw the duffle bag he had wrapped around his neck in the trunk. J-Murder had just given him some work to take to one of the stash cribs in the projects. When Wolverine pulled up in front of the building everything looked normal but once he stepped out and popped the trunk all he heard was "freeze". When Wolverine turned around he was staring down the barrel of Det. Ford's .357.

"Get on the fucking ground" Det. Ford yelled. Once Wolverine was on the ground Det. Ford quickly cuffed him and called for back up. The information Pooky had given him was correct and in return Det.

Ford was gonna give Pooky $100 for the info. Det. Ford found $6000 in Wolverine's pockets. He quickly took Wolverine's money and stuffed it in his pockets. "Don't worry about this you ain't gonna need it where your going" he said with a smirk on his face. Once the search was over he found two loaded 9mm and a duffle bag full of coke already bagged up. "Yeah it looks like your punk ass about to be doing some Fed time" Det. Ford said laughing as he put Wolverine in the backseat. "Now we gonna see how much Rico cares about you" Det. Ford said laughing as he pulled off and headed to the station.

* * *

Rico sat in his Escalade along with Peaches waiting for the light to change from red to green. Rico and Peaches had just come from the movies and were on their way to Peaches's crib to get their freak on. As Rico drove he never noticed the all black Buick that was following him instead he just continued driving listening to the sounds of Jay Z. As Rico stopped at another red light he looked in his side mirrors and noticed a car speeding up on him from the side with two men wearing hoodies hanging out the window. Rico was going to pull off but everything was happening too fast. Before Rico could pull off he was shook up by the loud sound of gunfire hitting his truck. Rico quickly ducked down and took cover as bullets came flying in. As shattered glass fell on top of Rico he took two shots to the back, luckily his bullet proof vest absorbed the shots. Once Rico felt two slugs hit him in his back he immediately pulled out his .45 threw his arm out the window and let off 5 rounds BOOM BOOM BOOM BOOM BOOM. One shot of Rico's four fifth hit one of the gunmen in his shoulder causing him to drop his Mac 10. Once the gunman dropped his ratchet the driver immediately stepped on the gas and pulled off. When Rico heard the gunmen pull off he quickly hopped out the whip and shot at the Buick until it disappeared. Rico stuck his smoking gun in his waistband and noticed Peaches sitting in the passenger seat with four holes in her chest and her eyes opened. "Damn Peaches I never meant for this to happen" Rico said checking Peaches's pulse. "Fuck"! Rico screamed as he heard the sirens. As the crowd started to gather around Rico jogged down the block and disappeared.

* * *

CHAPTER TWELVE

As soon as Wolverine made it to Rikers Island he hopped on the jack (phone) and called Rico. On the fifth ring Rico finally picked up.

"Yo who dis?"

"It's Wolverine"

"Where the fuck you been at" Rico asked.

"Nigga I'm on the island I been locked up for the last two days, that faggot ass cracker Det. Ford bagged me"

"How did he catch you?"

"J-Murder had just hit me off with the work and I was bringing it to the stash crib like I always do and as soon as I stepped out the whiThthis mufucka was right there waiting for me" Wolverine explained.

"Word, that shit sounds kind of funny something about that doesn't sound right"

"Yeah I know that clown Ford was trying to make me believe you ratted on me"

"Word?" Rico laughed.

"Yeah the nigga was saying you set me up thats how he knew when I would be holding mad work but I don't believe the nigga though. But anyway what's good wIth this bail money?"

"Nigga you ain't got no money saved up?"

"Nah son I ain't even got no money to get me a good lawyer" Wolverine lied.

"How much is ya bail?" Rico asked.

"A half a million dollars these mufuckas talking about I might have to do some Fed time" Wolverine said in a defeated tone.

"Well nigga I don't know what to tell you cause I ain't got no half a mill and I ain't got no properties to put up for ya bail so I don't know what to tell you" Rico said.

"What nigga you trying to play me cause I'm locked up, nigga you wouldn't even be where you at right now if it wasn't for me, now you gonna play me like some chump?" Wolverine snapped.

"Listen if I ain't got it what you want me to do?"

"Nigga don't play with me cause if that bitch Trina was locked up you would do whatever you had to do to get her up outta there"

"Listen fam this shit ain't got nothing to do with Trina" Rico said defensively.

"Oh I see you think shit is sweet cuz you home right?, you gonna see what time it is mufucka" Wolverine said hanging up in Rico's ear.

"Fuck that punk ass nigga" Rico thought. "If that bitch nigga ready for war all he gotta do is bring it that mufucka know where I'm at" Rico said out loud pouring himself a drink. Rico sat on the couch getting drunk watching New Jack City all day until he was interrupted by his cell phone. Rico looked at his caller ID and saw that it was Det. Lance. "Yeah what's up?"

"Why don't you tell me Rico?,I have not heard from you in a month and a half, what's going on?"

"I been mad busy B. I forgot all about our little deal" Rico said.

"Well I didn't mufucka you better come see me within the next 48 hours or else"

"Or else what?"

"Rico don't play with me if you ain't got that money then you gonna see how I get down" Det. Lance threatened.

"Listen Det. Lance I'm gonna come see you within the next 48 hours aight calm down you got my word"

"That's what I like to hear Rico I like you please stay on my good side trust me you don't wanna be on my bad side"

"Yeah whatever I'll call you when I get that paper ready" Rico hung up and finished getting his drink on. "Yo fuck that I'm bout kill this mufucka Det. Lance" Rico thought taking another sip from his drink. Fuck it why not? Rico was paying Det. Lance and Det. Lance wasn't even doing his part. "Aight that mufucka wanna take advantage of me, it's all good cuz I'm gonna go see dat clown in 48 hours but I'm gonna give him more then some paper" Rico said to himself before he dozed off on the couch.

***

Wolverine sat in his cell doing push ups thinking about how he was gonna get back at Rico. For the past 4 days all he could think about was how Rico was trying to play him.

"I don't believe I let this clown play me like this I should of took that nigga shit over when I had the fucking chance" Wolverine said getting up off the floor from doing his push ups. "A yo CO crack 16 cell" yelled Wolverine. Once the CO cracked Wolverine's cell he walked down the tear and gave the niggas he fucked with pounds. "I know this faggot ass nigga Rico set me up how else did the fucking jakes get the drop on me?" Wolverine thought as he walked down the tear. Wolverine knew it was only one way he was gonna get outta jail and he didn't care what he had to do, all he knew was that he was gonna kill Rico. Wolverine walked up and snatched the receiver outta the hands of some cornball ass nigga. "Yo money beat it before I lay ya ass out" Wolverine said to the guy as he hung up the phone and dialed his own number. On the sixth ring some cracker answered the phone. "Hello" "Yes can I speak to Det. Ford please?"

* * *

When Trina got released she was the happiest bitch in the world. Once the gates opened Trina ran out and hopped in Rico's Benz. "What's good Ma"? Rico asked with a big smile on his face.

"I'm just happy to be home" Trina said kissing Rico on the cheek.

"It's good to have you back B. word up ahad mad shit been going on"

"A lot of shit like what put me on" Trina said nosily.

"You know I'ma put you on but not right now, right now I just want you to relax and enjoy the good life" Rico said handing Trina a bottle of Moet. "Yo we got a little something planned for you for later on"

Trina smiled taking the bottle to the head.

"Let's do what we do" Rico said as he pulled off blasting Jadakiss new CD. The whole crew showed up at the Cherry Lounge to show Trina love. Rico set up a small celebration nothing big just family showing love and respect. Before the night was over Trina was throwing up for all the liquor she consumed. Rico gave J-Murder and the rest of the crew pounds as he helped Trina to the Benz. "Yo you better not throw up in my shit" Rico said as he got behind the wheel and pulled off.

* * *

Rico sat in Tiffany's Charger the next night screwing the silencer on his 9mm. Rico grabbed the book bag outta the passenger seat and headed in the building. Once the pissy elevator reached the 10th floor Rico walked down the hall until he reached the apartment he was looking for. After a few knocks Det. Lance answered the door. " Hey Rico how nice of you to finally show up" Det. Lance said stepping aside to let Rico in.

"Yeah I had a lot of running around to do earlier" Rico said sitting down on the couch.

"So how is everything going in the streets?" Lance asked.

"Same shit everyday you ain't making it no easier for me like you suppose to" Rico stated plainly.

"How you gonna say some shit like that I been doing the best I can, my only problem is that cocksucker Det. Ford that mufucka's been on my ass"! "Well if you can't produce then I don't see why I'm paying you, basically I'm paying for something I can't get to make a long story short you need to come up with another way to keep the jakes off me and my crew's back or else you ain't gonna see no more of my paper" Rico said raising his tone.

"Listen to me you dumb motherfucker I'm making sure no big heat is coming down on you and your crew, you talking about little bullshit uniform cops arresting you and your crew, mufucka I'm keeping the Feds off your ass boy now since you wanna bite the hand dat feeds you instead of $20,000 now I want $40,000 a month you ungrateful son of a bitch"

Rico sat on the couch ice grillin Det. Lance. "You know what you could do for me Det. Lance?"

"What?"

"You could suck my dick you faggot ass cracker" Rico said aiming his 9mm at Det. Lance's head.

"Hold on Rico think about what you are doing" Lance throwing his hands up in surrender.

"Think about what, I know what I'm doing you fucking pig, I'm about to make the world a better place" Rico said coldly.

"Wait Rico, I got $60,000 in the back room it's yours just please don't do this" Det. Lance said begging for his life.

"Listen B I gotta make moves I ain't got time for this bullshit yo have a nice day" PST PST PST PST Rico said leaving 4 bullets in Det. Lance head. Rico threw Det. Lance's $60,000 in his book bag and left the crime scene.

***

Tiffany sat on the couch with Heather watching videos. When Tiffany got up to get something to eat she felt something wet dripping down her leg. "Oh shit my water broke" she said to herself. Tiffany ran to the phone and called the ambulance. Once she hung up the phone she called Rico. "I'm about to have the baby, I just called the ambulance"

"Aight what hospital you going to?" Rico asked excitedly.

"I'm going to Harlem Hospital and I'm taking Heather wit me" she said ending the call.

"Tiff just called and said she about to have the baby" Rico said giving J-Murder and Buck both pounds.

"Congratulations mufucka" Buck said spraying champagne all over his basement floor. When the trio made it outside J-Murder pulled out his P89 and bust two shots in the air "my mufuckin nigga about to be a daddy" he screamed as they all hopped in Buck's Expedition and peeled off.

Married To Da Streets

Tiffany laid on the hospital bed in pain. "Where the fuck is Rico at" she wondered. Not even a minute later Rico came walking in her room with a camcorder in one hand and a whole bunch of balloons in the other. "Hey baby what's up?"

"I thought something happened to you Rico"

"Come on Ma what I told you about stressing with my baby in ya stomach, you know I wouldn't miss dis for the world". Rico and Tiffany's conversation was interrupted when Trina walked in with Janet.

"Hey son Trina told me ya girlfriend was about to have the baby tonight so you know I wasn't gonna miss my first grandchild being born. Anyway how have you been Rico, you know I missed you right?" Janet said.

"I came to check on you a few times but you wasn't home" Rico said putting down the camcorder. His Mom's was looking real good Rico could tell she had got off the drugs and was getting her shit together.

"Oh I'm sorry I wasn't home but I've been real busy at work lately, oh fuck that come here Baby" Janet said giving Rico a big hug.

"Damn Ma you look real good" Rico said hugging his mother. Four hours later Tiffany gave birth to a beautiful baby girl. Rico and Tiffany sat up all night watching little Yasira sleep.

"Damn she looks just like you" Rico said stroking Tiffany's hair.

"Now that you a father you know you got to slow down right?" Tiffany said looking into Rico's eyes.

"Yeah Ma I know what I gotta do and trust and believe I'm never gonna leave this pretty little girl's side no matter what. Whatever I gotta do I'ma do it" Rico said.

"Oh so what about me?" Tiffany said. "you don't care if you leave my side?"

"Stop being so jealous all the time you know I ain't ever gonna leave neither one of you so fix ya face" Rico said kissing her on the cheek. The two sat up all night talking about their new little princess.

***

Buck pulled up in front of the Chinese restaurant with Chyna bumping some Jay Z. Chyna was a " jump off" one of Buck's hoes that he got down with from time to time. The only reason he fucked with her was cause she was a down ass bitch. Whether he needed her to transport some work, hold a burner, and suck his dick or whatever Chyna was down for the cause.

"Ma I want an order of fry chicken wings and pork fried rice and make sure they put some ketchup on the chicken and don't forget the duck sauce either" Buck said.

"I know how you like it already" Chyna said closing the car door. Buck took another pull on his blunt. As Buck sat waiting for Chyna to come out the Chinese restaurant he saw this brolick cat who looked unfamiliar. "Yo where the fuck do I know dis nigga from?" Buck asked himself staring at the big man. "Oh shit thats that mufucka Cali be with" Buck said pulling out his .40 caliber. Chyna came out the Chinese restaurant with Buck's food and hopped back in the whip.

"Chyna I need you to do me a favor, walk up on the passenger side of that truck and distract the driver, make sure you get that mufucka's full attention"

"I got you baby" Chyna said as she went to go handle her business. Hulk sat in his Yukon looking for a CD to put on when his train of thought was interrupted when a bad dark skin chick appeared at his side window.

"What's up Shorty?" Hulk asked liking what he saw.

"I don't mean to bother you, but can I use ya cell phone for a minute, my girlfriend was supposed to pick me up about 20 minutes ago and she ain't here yet" Chyna said.

"I can give you a ride if you want" Hulk said getting ready to lay his game down.

"Cool let me just call my girl and let her know dat I already got a ride" Chyna said.

Hulk passed Chyna the cell phone picturing how he was gonna fuck the shit out of her in his mind.

When Buck saw that Chyna had his undivided attention he made his move. Buck slowly crept up to the driver's side of the truck. "A yo my man"! When Hulk turned around he knew he had been played. Buck looked into his eyes and let the .40 caliber spit BOOM BOOM BOOM was all that could be heard along with shattering glass followed by a few screams. After Buck popped Hulk's top him and Chyna hopped in the whip and peeled off.

***

Rico and J-Murder sat in the hood shooting the breeze making sue their workers were on they job, when Trina pulled up. From the way Trina was looking Rico knew something was wrong.

"What's good?" Rico asked giving Trina a kiss on the cheek.

"I just came from seeing this nigga Pee Wee to pick up some paper and that clown talking about he ain't paying nothing until he talks to you" Trina said clearly upset.

"You talking about Pee Wee from Grant projects?" Rico asked.

"Yeah that bum ass nigga" Trina said with an attitude.

"Aight don't worry I'm gonna take care of that shit "Rico said laughing. The three sat and had a few laughs until it started raining. "A yo I'm gonna catch up wit ya'll niggas B, I'm about to go pick up that paper from Pee Wee" Rico said giving J-Murder and Trina a pound before he hopped in the charger to get out the rain.

"What's good my nigga?" Pee Wee asked as he hopped in the passenger seat.

"You tell me what's up, Trina said you was giving her a hard time wit that paper what's up wit that?"

"Nah it ain't even like that, I just wanted to hit you off myself you know what I'm saying. I don't do business like dat" Pee Wee said handing Rico $5000.

"I respect that" Rico said stuffing the $5000 in his pockets. " But check this out, I can't be running around just cause a mufucka wanna deal with me only, know what I'm saying? I be having mad shit to do next time just deal with whoever I send cause you know I ain't gonna send no cornball ass niggon smell me?"

"Yeah I smell you but yo I gotta make moves B and I need 200 grams" Pee Wee said pulling out a knot (a lot of money).

"Prices done went up to 35 now" Rico said.

"35?" Pee Wee repeated. "What I look like some down south nigga or something?"

"Listen son it's a drought right now" Rioc told him. "What you think I'm trying to play you or something, matter of fact you want it or not?"

"Yeah I'ma take it" Pee Wee said not feeling how Rico raised the price on him. Rico sold Pee Wee 200 grams and went on about his business.

As Rico was driving he suddenly slammed on his brakes. "Yo I know thats not that mufucka Kenny?" Rico said looking through his wet windshield. "Hell yeah thats that bitch ass nigga" Rico said creeping up on Kenny. When Kenny went to cross the street Rico stepped on the gas and hit Kenny with the car. Rico then quickly hopped out the whip with his gun drawn and ran up on Kenny. "Get up you bitch ass nigga" Rico yelled as he broke Kenny's nose with theburner (gun). "I give you an inch and you take a mile from me" Rico said hitting Kenny one more time with the gun. Rico then went and popped the trunk, it was raining so hard Rico could barely see. "Come here mufucka" Rico said violently grabbing Kenny by the collar.

"Come on baby we family don't do this" Kenny said copping a plea.

"Shut up you should have thought about that shit before you crossed the line" Rico said throwing Kenny in the trunk. Once Kenny was in the trunk Rico got behind the wheel and took off.

Married To Da Streets

When the trunk finally opened Kenny saw J-Murder and Bull aiming their guns at his head. "Don't fucking move" Bull said as he handcuffed Kenny's hands behind his back and dragged him inside the warehouse. When Kenny saw Rico standing in the abandoned warehouse holding a Mac 10 he damn near shitted on himself. "Come on baby don't do this we supposed to be family". Rico just pointed the Mac in his uncle's direction and tore his ass up, riddling his body with bullets. "Yo make sure ya'll niggas take care of this nigga's body" Rico said to J-Murder and Bull as he broke out.

Rico walked in his bedroom and saw Tiffany lying on the bed wearing some lace panties and a wife beater. "What's up baby"? Rico asked kissing Tiffany's lips.

"I know you better stop talking so loud before you wake the baby up" Tiffany huffed.

"Shit fuck waking the baby up, as good as you look right now we about to make another one" Rico said playfully as he tried to pull Tiffany's panties off.

"What you think you doing?" Tiffany said stopping him. "You know we can't have sex until I Fully recover from having this baby"

"Aw shit I forgot all about dat shit, just let me get a little bit I won't hurt you" Rico joked.

"Boy you must be crazy you ain't getting none of this pussy but I know something you can have" Tiffany said as she unbuckled Rico's belt.

Tiffany could see in Rico's facyouthat he was stressed out and had a lot o n his mind so for the rest of the night she gave him slow neck until it wasn't a drop of cum left in his dick.

The next morning Rico woke up to his cell phone ringing, he looked at the caller Id and saw that it was Buck. "What's good my boy?"

"Chilling yo I'm in Atlanta right now"

"Why what's up?" Rico asked.

"I had to merk that big nigga Hulk the other day"

"You talking about the nigga that be wit Cali"

"Yeah I had to pop that nigga top but the word on the streets is the jakes is looking for me so they can question me so I said fuck that I'm gonna come back to Atl until the heat dies down a little bit you know what I mean?"

"I feel you but who's holding the spot down?" Rico asked.

"That nigga Bull holding it down right now but what's good we could start making some moves down here. My niggas already got a spot out here but you know them down south niggas don't know how to get it like niggas from up top. So if you wanna make this happen all you gotta do is say the word" Buck said.

"I tell you what we gonna do me and Trina gonna come out there and set shit up then after everything is set up ya peoples can take it from there. Just make sure every week they send us some paper and I ain't got no problem making this shit happen" Rico said thinking about all the money that was about to be made.

"No problem it's about time we start expanding anyway"

"Yeah I know me and Trina gonna come out there in like three days and get shit poppin, oh yeah and good looking for taking care of that big dumb nigga"

"Don't worry about it it's nothing just holla at me when ya'll on your way out here, you heard?"

"I got you say no more"

***

Trina hopped on the Greyhound heading to Atlanta with half a brick and 20 pounds of weed in her bag that was held under the bus. While Trina was on the bus Rico was driving a Nissan he rented. Before Rico left the hood he left J-Murder in charge of everything. He also hired this killer named Trigger to watch over Tiffany while he was gone just in case Cali tried to get back at him for killing Hulk. Rico made sure that nobody knew what was going on but him and Trigger. Trigger's job was to follow Tiffany everywhere she went without her even knowing she was being followed and to make sure nothing happened to her.

***

CHAPTER THIRTEEN

Wolverine sat in McDonald's with Rocks and Sticks. Rocks and Sticks weren't the Feds instead they were two of Brooklyn's finest stick up kids. Rocks and Sticks didn't like how Rico had brushed them off that night at the restaurant so when Wolverine came to them with a plan to take Rico out of business they were more then willing to help him out.

"Yo when we finish with him he ain't gonna know what hit him" Wolverine said stuffing his mouth with chicken nuggets.

"Yeah son I wanna make that nigga Rico suffer, yo I can't stand when a nigga start getting money then start shitting on niggas like he better then niggas and shit" Rocks said sipping on his juice.

"Yo fuck all that once this nigga is history we gonna take over his spot and shut shit down".

"I heard the crillz (crack) be moving like crazy over there" Sticks said.

"Shit definitely be moving over there" Wolverine said confidently. " Everything gonna be good cuz all the fiends know me over there already me so we ain't got to worry about all that all we gotta worry about is Rico and all of his yes men" Wolverine said as the three men finished their meal.

***

Rico and Buck set shit up lovely down south. Shit was moving and everybody was happy. All the down south country niggas was sweating Trina. They loved how she dressed and how she talked. Every guy Trina looked hooked up with Rico robbed them and when they came they came correct. Everything was going smooth in the hood so Trina, Rico, and Buck decided to head over to club "Fuel" and get their party on. Rico stuck his .22 in his Timbs as the three hopped in Buck's Range Rover. Rico knew he couldn't bring his hammer (gun) in the club how he did in New York. But fuck that the deuce was better then nothing. Rico didn't care how but he was definitely getting in the club with his .22. Rico sat in the passenger seat when he decided to call his crib. After 8 rings the answering machine picked up. Instead of leaving a message Rico just hung up. "Where the fuck is this bitch at?" Rico thought. "Fuck it I'll call her when I get up out the club" he said to himself listening to Sheek's CD. When Buck pulled up in front of the club it was nothing but mad niggas hanging out on the strip and even more beautiful ladies hanging on the strip. As soon as Rico stepped out the whip he had all the ladies attention, the minute he stepped out the truck. Everybody knew he wasn't from there just from his outfit.

Once inside the club Rico copped three bottles of Moet and headed to the VIP section. Through Out the night Rico had bitches draped all over him. Before the night was over Rico knew who he was gonna fuck that night. He had his eyes on this shorty name Cookie. Cookie was dark skin with a nice weave, some big tities and a big ole country ass.

"Damn she got the wild fatty" Rico said watching Cookie shake her ass to the beat. After 3 hours of bounce music a fight finally broke out in the middle of the dance floor. When the bouncers broke up the fight Rico decided it was time to leave. Rico walked up to Trina and handed her his .22. "Yo I'm about to breeze wit this shorty" he said pointing to Cookie. Rico kissed Trina's cheek and gave Buck a pound. "Yo ya'll be careful up in here B. "Rico said before him and Cookie disappeared in the crowd. Rico and Cookie hopped in her Mazda and went straight to her crib.

Once in her crib Cookie gave Rico a tour of her one bedroom apartment. When the two reached Cookie's bedroom they were all over each other. Cookie desperately pulled out Rico's dick and threw it in her mouth. She massaged and sucked on Rico's dick until Rico came and she swallowed every last one of Rico's babies. Cookie continued to suck on Rico's dick until he was ready for round two. Cookie then kicked her heels off and slid out of her jeans. When Rico saw that ass in a thong he quickly threw on a condom and snatched Cookie's thong off. Cookie got on all 4's on the bed and looked at Rico. "Come get this pussy" she said in her sexiest voice. Rico palmed both of Cookie's ass cheeks as he slid up inside her.

"Ahww" Cookie moaned as she felt his dick in her stomach. "Yeah thats how I like it" she moaned as she threw the ass back at Rico. All Cookies' moaning was turning Rico on. The louder she moaned the deeper he went. Rico watched Cookie's ass jiggle all over the place with every stroke. He slapped Cookie's ass. "This shit is all yours" she screamed loving every stroke. Cookie then jumped up and pushed Rico on his back, she planted both of her feet on the bed and hopped on Rico's dick and rode it like a wild bull. Rico then pulled Cookie on her back and started long stroking her. "Ahw yes fuck me baby" Cookie screamed as she wrapped her legs around Rico's waist and dug her nails in his back. Rico stroked Cookie's fat wet juicy pussy until he finally came. After Rico finished digging Cookie's back out he hopped in the shower. When he got out Cookie lotioned him up and gave him a nice hot oil massage. Rico fucked the shit out of Cookie for the rest of the night until the sun rose. The next morning Cookie made Rico breakfast before she dropped Rico off in the hood. Rico and Cookie exchanged numbers and Rico promised to give her a call. He kissed Cookie on the cheek and headed to the building Buck was standing at. When Rico walked in the crib he saw Trina and Buck counting stacks of money. "What's good" Rico said giving them both pounds.

"All work and no play" Trina said as if she was jealous.

"Let me find out" Buck said laughing.

"Nigga please Rico is like my brother" Trina said defending herself.

"Yo my niggas should be finished wit everything by tomorrow morning but before I breeze I'ma go see Cookie one more time" Rico thought to himself as he took a long drag on the blunt.

***

Wolverine pulled up in the projects in an all black Ford Explorer along with Rocks and Sticks blasting some new Jadakiss shit. "I'ma show ya'll little niggas how to do this shit" Wolverine said pulling out 2 Berettas. "Ya'll niggas better not freeze up either"

"Nigga we does this" Rocks said cocking his Desert Eagle. The three gunmen threw on their hoodies and ran up in the building. Googles stood in the staircase serving mad crack heads. "Yo what's up I got $ 18 let me get two" Pooky begged.

"Yo you holding up the line if you ain't got enough money get the fuck out the line" Goggles said screaming on Pooky. Pooky and Goggles was caught off guard when the staircase door swung open and three men wearing hoodies came running in. Sticks immediately cracked Goggles in the head with his .357 and violently threw him on the pissy staircase floor. All the fiends ran up out the staircase. But before Pooky could get out the staircase Wolverine grabbed him by the back of the neck and laid him out with one hit from his 9mm.

"Yo gimme the keys to the stash crib on the 11th floor" Wolverine said pointing his 9mm at Goggle's head. Without hesitation Goggles tossed Wolverine the keys. "Yo take care of that" Wolverine said handing Rocks the keys.

"11th floor apartment # C" Wolverine then took all Goggle's crack and money. " Oh shit you shining too? Nigga gimme that shit" Wolverine said snatching Goggle's chain from around his neck.

"Nigga run all that shit" Sticks said taking Goggle's pinky ring, watch, and bracelet.

"Wolverine I thought we was cool why are you doing this?" Goggle's asked holding the big ass knot on his head.

"Nigga this is business and you already know business is business, now the shit with me and Rico is personal nigga. You just at the wrong place at the wrong time". After Wolverine and Sticks took all of Goggles shit Pooky woke up screaming. "What's going on?"

"Nigga you better shut the fuck up before I pop ya fucking head off" Wolverine said aiming his 9mm at Pooky's head.

"Wolverine thats you?" Pooky asked as his vision started coming back. "What's all this about?"

"Nigga you thought I wasn't gonna find out you snitched on me?"

"Nah Wolverine you see what had happened was...."

"Shut the fuck up" Wolverine screamed as he slapped Pooky with the toast. Seconds later Rocks came running down the stairs with two duffle bags on his shoulders. "I got everything let's be out" he said out of breath. Wolverine immediately pointed his 9mm at Pooky's head and pulled the trigger sending the scrawny crack head flying down the stairs. Once Sticks saw Wolverine pop the crack head he put 5 bullets in Goggles chest. The three gunmen then he left the building as if nothing had happened.

***

Rico made it home and realized no one was there. "Yo what the fuck this bitch ain't been home since I left" Rico said getting mad and jealous at the same time. "This bitch gonna make me bust her fucking head open" Rico said pulling out his cell phone, on the third ring a man with a deep voice answered.

"Yo my nigga Trigger what's poppin"? "Ain't shit I'm downtown keeping my eye on Tiffany".

"Yo where the fuck she been since I been gone?" Rico asked.

"Her and Heather is shopping right now but for the last week she been with some stocky cat, with mad waves in his head" Trigger told him.

"A stocky cat?, does the nigga drive a black Impala?"

"Yeah thats him"

"Damn she creeping wit my man J-Murder, I'ma kill both of them mufuckas" Rico thought right before Trigger interrupted his thoughts.

"Yo you still want me to continue following this broad?"

"Yeah keep me updated on what's going on, oh yeah where's my daughter?"

"Oh Tiffany dropped her off at ya Mom's crib" Trigger said

"Aight I'ma holla at you keep me posted on what's poppin".

When Rico hung up the phone he was ready to kill J-Murder, he had already gave Chyna the work to take to Atlanta for Buck so he had plenty of time to think of plan. Rico decided to play dumb and see if Tiffany or J-Murder would come and tell him what was going on. Rico picked up his cell phone, and dialed J-Murder's number. "Yo what's good son?"

"You back in New York?" J-Murder asked.

"Yeah why what's up?" Rico asked suspiciously.

"Yo meet me at I HOPS I gotta holla at you about something"

"Aight I'm on my way".

Rico pulled out his .380 and screwed the silencer on. "I'm gonna pop this nigga head off if he tells me he fucked my wife and betrayed me" Rico said as he stuck the .380 in his waistband and hopped in the Benz.

When Rico made it to I HOPS J-Murder was already there waiting for him.

"What's good my boy"? Rico said giving J Murder a pound and sat down. "So what's poppin? What's been going on since I left?"

"Shit been crazy out here B, somebody hit our stash crib, them mufuckas got us for $ 80,000, 30 pounds of weed and a half a brick" J-Murder informed him.

"Fuck, were you at when this shit went down?" Rico asked already knowing the answer.

"I was in the Bronx picking up that paper from that nigga Bull" J-Murder lied. "Oh yeah and whoever hit up our spot killed Goggles, and Pooky"

"So you telling me nobody know nothing?" Rico said getting madder and madder by the second. "Yo what's up you heard anything from dat nigga Cali?"

"Nah I think the nigga got the fucking message" J-Murder said sipping on some water.

"Listen B I gotta go take care of something B make sure we don't take no one loses in these streets cuz we can't afford it right now you hear me. Get on ya fucking job B" Rico said as he gave J murder a pound and hopped in his Benz.

Rico went straight to Kim's crib so he could get a piece of mind and just relax. Kim gave him a nice long massage and followed it up with some slow neck. Rico sat on the couch sipping some Belve thinking about what he should do, too much shit was happening to fast. Rico had enough money to just get up outta New York and never come back but he just couldn't leave. He loved the streets, he loved everything about the streets. The streets were all he knew getting money, fucking bitches, punching niggas in the mouth, and popping guns is all Rico knew and he wasn't changing for nobody.

Rico sat on the couch watching "Paid In Full" with Kim when higo cell phone started ringing. Rico looked at his caller ID and saw it was Tiffany. "Yo what up?"

"Where you at?" She asked.

"I'm chillin where the fuck you been at?"

"Me and Heather went shopping, damn what's wrong wit you?" Tiffany said crumbling up her face.

"Ain't nothing wrong with me I'll be home in a little while aight"

When Rico hung up his cell phone Kim was looking dead in his face. "I know that bitch ain't playing herself?" She said in a nasty tone.

"Nah we just going through something right now thats all" Rico said down playing it.

"Well that bitch better be treating you like a fucking king cause if she ain't I'm going over there and tighten her ass up" Kim said.

"Listen Ma just be easy it ain't dat serious"

"Shit to you it's not but to me it is that serious, she ya wife and I'm not but I gotta respect that cause she met you first and ya'll got some time in it together but let that bitch get out of line" Kim said looking like a maniac.

"Damn you look so sexy when you get mad "Rico said placing one of Kim's nice size breasts in his mouth.

"You better stop acting like I won't kill a bitch for you" Kim said letting out a soft moan. Rico slowly undressed Kim and kissed her from head to toe. He then turned Kim over and hit her with the drunk dick. The louder Kim screamed the deeper Rico went all that could be heard was Kim screaming out in extasy. Rico's torso slapping against Kim's ass and pussy making a loud wet sound squishing sound. Rico tore that pussy up and put Kim straight to sleep.

***

CHAPTER FOURTEEN

Cali went to L.A. to spend some time with his wife Simone. It had been about 3 months since the two saw each other. Cali and Simone made love for 4 hours straight. That's just what Cali needed to see his wife and get his mind right. Cause he knew when he got back to New York he was gonna need a clear mind to take out Rico. "I got something for his ass" Cali said as he held Simone for the rest of the night.

***

For the last couple of days Tiffany noticed Rico wasn't acting like himself, it just seemed like something was bothering him. Every time she asked him was everything alright he would respond and say "why don't you tell me?" Tiffany didn't know what to do. "Hopefully he'll like the surprise birthday me and J-Murder are throwing for him in two weeks" Tiffany said to herself and finished cleaning up the house.

***

When Buck arrived at LaGuardia Airport Trina and Rico were sitting in Trina's Lex waiting on him. Buck hopped in the LexUs that had Young

Jeezy blasting through the speakers. "What's good my niggas" he said giving both Trina and Rico a pound. "What's up, we about to hit This club you rollin?" Rico asked.

"Yeah why not I ain't got shit else to do" Buck said bobbing his head to the music.

The club was packed like always and everybody was dressed to impress. Rico sat in the VIP section with some chick draped all over him while Trina sat in VIP getting her drink on. Buck on the other hand was on the dance floor shaking his money maker. Rico sat in VIP getting a lap dance from some thick chick with a short hair cut. "Damn this bitch working dat shit" Rico said as he gripped the young woman's hips. At the end of the night everybody exited the club and just stood outside shooting the breeze. Everything was going fine, Rico was hollering at the thick chick who gave him a lap dance while Buck was laying his game down to some dark skin shorty and Trina was talking on her cell phone. As Rico was getting the cuties phone number he saw a big strong looking guy pulling on Trina's arm.

"Yo Ma you looking mad good, I'm saying what's really good?" The big drunk man said pulling on Trina's arm.

"Thanks for the compliment but I already got a man" Trina said trying to pull away from the man's grip.

"But I'm saying Ma you wearing them jeans tho" the man slurred.

"Listen let my arm go before you regret it" Trina warned.

"Bitch I'm trying to make ya day" the man said louder then he intended to.

When Rico saw the shit getting outta of control he stepped in. "A yo my man is there a problem over here?" Rico asked looking the diesel nigga in his eyes.

"Yo mind ya business son" the big man said as he let Trina's arm go and faced Rico.

"Yo money check this out....". Before Rico could get his words out his mouth. The big man had stole on him. The impact from the punch caused Rico to hit the floor but he wasn't knocked out. The big man then started to kick Rico in the ribs while he was down. As the big man continued to kick Rico, Trina jumped on his back and started choking him. The big man immediately flung Trina over his shoulder and violently threw her to the ground. When Rico saw Trina's body hit the ground like a rag doll, he pulled out his .45 and popped the big man three times in the stomach. As Rico let off the last shot he saw two police officers running in his direction. Rico quickly tossed the gun and took off running. After a block and a half of running the cops tackled Rico and then threw the cuffs on him. When the cops were chasing Rico, Buck saw Rico toss the burner. Buck picked up the hot gun stuck it in the small of his back as him and Trina left the crime scene. Ten minutes later it was about a thousand cops on the scene including Det.

Ford. Det. Ford opened up the back door of the police car and smiled when he saw Rico handcuffed and sitting in the backseat.

"Didn't I tell you that I was going to get you? You done fucked up big time and I'm gonna make sure you don't see the light of day again you filthy cocksucker" Det. Ford said as he took a step back and hog spit in Rico's face.

* * *

Tiffany rolled over and picked up the house phone that was ringing off the hook. She looked at the alarm clock that read 4:40 am as she spoke. "Who this?"

"Trina yo wake up Rico just got locked up"

When Tiffany heard that she jumped up and threw on anything as she continued to ask questions. "Trina what happened?"

"Some guy was getting real disrespectful and swung on me and Rico shot him"

"So where is he right now?" Tiffany asked.

"I don't know get dressed and meet me in front of my building and while ya on your way I'll find out where he's at" Trina said as she hung up the phone. Tiffany got dressed threw her hair in a ponytail got little Yasira dressed and flew out the door. Tiffany pulled up in front of Trina's building and Trina was right there waiting for her. "Yo they got him at the 34th precinct" Trina said hopping in the passenger seat.

When Trina and Tiffany walked up in the police station the crackers were being very disrespectful. "Yes excuse me I would like to know if you bought in a gentleman by the name of Rico Anderson?"Tiffany asked very politely.

"Hey go sit over there and I'll be there in a minute" the cop barked in a very nasty tone. Instead of flipping out on the nasty cracker, Tiffany just walked over to the benches and started patting Yasira on her back softly as her and Trina took a seat on the hard bench. An hour later Trina couldn't take it anymore she walked up to the desk and screamed on the fat nasty cracker. "Excuse me but we been sitting over there waiting for you to get back to us. Now do you have a man back there by the name of Rico Anderson or not!?"

"Oh yeah Rico Anderson they just sent him to the bookings 5 minutes ago" said the Redneck.

"Mufucka you had us sitting over here all that time and now you gonna tell us you shipped him out 5 minutes ago, when we been sitting over there a mufuckin hour" Tiffany huffed.

"Mam calm down"

"No fuck you and the rest of these crackers I can't stand all ya'll salty mufuckas" Trina barked as her and Tiffany walked up out the station heated. The next day Tiffany and Trina sat in the courtroom all day waiting for them to call Rico's name. When they finally called Rico's name he came out with his lawyer and the judge said he didn't come up with a bail for Rico yet and told him to come back next week. So after all those hours of waiting Trina and Tiffany only got to see Rico for 40 seconds. But as Rico walked back to the bull pin Rico mouthed the words "I'ma call you" to Tiffany as the officer escorted him to the back.

***

The next day Wolverine sat staked out watching Buck's crack house. "Damn they got shit clicking over here" Wolverine said to himself as he kept his eyes close on the scene. After hours of waiting patiently Wolverine saw Bull come out the building across the street from the crack house and hop in a bull shit Honda Accord. Bull drove a couple of blocks and stopped at a Spanish restaurant. Wolverine hopped out the all white Jetta and stood right next to the door. Ten minutes later Bull walked up out of the restaurant not even aware of what was going down. Bull continued to walk to his car until he felt some steel on his back.

"Listen you already know what time it is just be cool and walk over to the white car" Wolverine said with one arm around Bull's shoulder and the other one clutching the 9mm he held to Bull's ribs. "Yo get in the front seat you driving mufucka" Wolverine said as Bull got in the driver's seat and he got in the backseat. When they finally reached their destination Bull saw two men walking up to the vehicle. Rocks opened up the driver's door carrying a roll of duck tap. "Mufucka don't look stupid you already know how it's going down" he said as he taped Bull's hands behind his back. Rocks and Sticks escorted Bull to Rock's basement.

"Ok now I'm only asking you dis once" Wolverine said circling Bull's chair. "Where is the stash crib?"

"Wolverine why are you doing this?" Bull asked not understanding what was going on.

"What the fuck is this 21 questions mufucka this my last time asking you, where the fuck is the stash crib" Wolverine said putting a bullet in both of Bull's knee caps.

"Aw shit" Bull screamed out in pain "yo it's across the street from the crack house he confessed. Once Rocks and Sticks wrote down the directions and took the keys from Bull's pocket and went to handle their business.

***

Buck sat in Chyna's crib watching her head bob up and down on his dick. "Damn Ma handle ya business" Buck said grabbing the back of Chyna's head. Chyna deep throated Buck's dick until he exploded in her mouth. Once Chyna finished handling her business she made Buck a sandwich. "Yo good looking Chyna I gotta go handle some business. I'ma come back and see you as soon as I'm done" Buck said as he kissed Chyna on the cheek as he headed out the door. Buck pulled up to the stash crib across the street and made his way to the apartment. Buck opened the door and could tell something was wrong the moment he looked inside. Buck slowly walked throughout the living room with his P89 drawn. When he finally made it to the back room he saw the big floor model safe wide open and empty as a whistle. Buck then walked over to the closet and noticed that the closet was empty. "What the fuck" all the money, drugs, and guns were missing. Buck knew him, Bull, and Rico were the only three who knew about this stash crib. "Rico couldn't have did it cuz he's in jail" Buck said to himself meaning it could only be Bull. Buck pulled out his cell phone.

***

Wolverine sat in Rock's basement watching Rocks and Sticks continue to torture Bull. Wolverine sat at the table dividing all the money Rocks and Sticks had just bought back when he heard Bull's cell phone start to ring. "Who the fuck you got calling you?" Wolverine asked snatching Bull's cell phone off his waist. "Yo who this?"

"Yo where's Bull?" Buck asked.

"Who is this punk ass Buck?"Wolverine asked knowing who it was.

"Yeah dis Buck who this?"

"Nigga you talking to the boss, this Wolverine nigga and I got your punk ass friend over here crying like a bitch"

"Wolverine?" Buck asked dumbfounded. "What's this all about?"

"Nigga I ain't got time to be answering a whole bunch of fucking questions, ask that bitch ass nigga Rico what it's all about"

"Listen Wolverine I don't know what's going on between you and Rico but yo just be easy before you start a war" Buck said.

"Nigga the war already started you bitch ass nigga matter of fact" POW POW POW. Wolverine shot bull in the chest three times! "Now the war is on whether you like it or not" Wolverine said hanging up in Buck's ear.

***

Rico walked through the visiting room doors and saw Tiffany sitting there waiting for him with a smile on her face. "Hey Daddy I missed you so much" she said holding Rico tight in her arms. "How they treating you baby?"

"I'm alright I talked to my lawyer and he said he got me a bail for $ 400,000 so this what I want you to do, go and tell Trina to drop that paper off to my lawyer and he's gonna put up the property". Rico could see in Tiffany's eyes that she was happy about the news.

"So baby you know ya birthday is next week, what you wanna do?" Tiffany asked excitedly.

"To tell you the truth I ain't even thinking about no birthday right now I got mad shit on my mind" Rico exhaled.

"Don't worry about it baby cause when you come home I'm gonna take all ya worries away and clear ya head right on up" Tiffany said giving Rico her sexy smirk.

"I should be home in two days, oh yeah and the lawyer said the clown that I shot didn't die so dats good news. I rather have an attempt murder charge, then a murder charge any day"

"Baby don't worry about nothing you gonna beat this case so don't even stress it them crackers ain't even got the fucking gun, no gun, no witnesses, no case" Tiffany smiled.

"Baby I hope you right"

"Everything is gonna be fine" Tiffany said giving Rico a big hug and a long kiss.

"Yo I'ma call you later baby" Rico said slapping Tiffany on the ass.

"I love you don't forget to call me" Tiffany said walking through the exit.

Rico sat in the dayroom playing Spades when he remembered to call Buck. When Rico got to the phones it was two guys already using them. "A yo my man let me see that jack (phone) when you finish" Rico said to the bald head brother that was using it. Twenty minutes the bald guy tapped Rico on the shoulder to let him know he was off the phone. Rico picked up the phone and called Tiffany. First they talked for about 10 minutes then he hung up and called Buck on the fourth ring Buck finally picked up. "Hello?"

"Yo what's good my boy?"

"You ain't gonna believe what happened" Buck said.

"What?"

"That nigga Wolverine just killed Bull and hit up the crack house, the nigga talking about he wanna go to war wit you and shit, yo let me know what's good cause I'm ready to put that work in on this clown"

"Just be easy I can't really talk on dis phonem Just fall back, I'll be home in two days, once I come home we will take it from there"

As Rico was talking on the phone he looked to his right and saw some clown ass nigga looking all in his mouth. "Yo money what's good, you lost something over here?" Before the guy could even fix his mouth to say something Rico had hit the man in his head with the phone knocking him out cold. Rico then began to stomp the man out until the riot squad came and beat him down with their night sticks and sent him to the box.

***

Two days later Rico was finally released him and Tiffany went straight to their house to spend some quality time together. The night before Tiffany dropped Yasira and Heather off at Janet's house so now she and Rico had the whole crib to themselves. As soon as the two stepped foot in the house Tiffany was all over Rico, kissing him and ripping off his clothes. Rico finally took control of the situation. Rico slid Tiffany's thong to the side and dropped to his knees as Tiffany threw one leg up on the couch. Rico dove in head first and licked and sucked on Tiffany's favorite spot. Rico ate Tiffany's pussy like the shit was going out of style. With every lick he had Tiffany's body going crazy until finally Tiffany couldn't take it anymore and let out what she had been holding in for the few days. After Rico finished eating Tiffany's pussy she couldn't wait to feel Rico inside of her. Tiffany grabbed Rico's arm and led him by the wall in the living room. She then placed both hands on the wall, bent over and spread her legs. Rico went right up in her from behind nice and slow. Rico long stroked Tiffany until her pussy juices were running down her thighs. "Who pussy is dis"? Rico asked speeding up his strokes. "Daddy dis pussy is all yours" she moaned as Rico continued to dig her out. Rico made love to Tiffany in every position until they both passed out on the couch.

Later on that night J-Murder and Rico sat at a red light waiting for it to change. "Yo son we been looking for this mufucka all night" Rico said passing the blunt to J-Murder.

"Yeah I know son I'm starving right now"

"Fuck it let's go get some Popeye's and call it a night" said Rico. "Don't worry Wolverine I'm coming for ya ass believe that" Rico said to himself as he turned up the volume and pushed the seat back.

***

Wolverine pulled up in front of Popeye's in his Range Rover sitting on 22's blasting some new Killa Cam. Wolverine double parked and stepped out the truck " glittering" his chain, bracelet, watch, earrings, and pinky ring were glowing in the dark. Wolverine walked in Popeye's along with one of his flunkies and stared at the menu until his thoughts were interrupted by the punk ass cashier standing behind the glass. "Hello may I take your order?"

"Yeah you can start by giving me 15 pieces of chicken mufucka and I want all breast to and I want Uhm..."

"Will that be all sir?"

"Yo stop interrupting me mufucka gimme 15 pieces of chicken, 5 biscuits, 4 orders of fries, and 2 ice teas you bitch ass nigga" Wolverine said making a scene. "Yo dis faggot ass nigga gonna make me fuck around and clap his ass" Wolverine said giving his flunky a pound.

"That will be $25.67 sir" the cashier said looking nervous even though he was protected by the bullet proof glass in front of him.

"Yo keep the change you clown ass nigga" Wolverine said slipping $30 through the glass.

"Okay sir your food will be ready in about 5 minutes".

Wolverine sat talking to his flunky when three beautiful dark skin women came walking up in the spot. "Damn ladies where the party at?" Wolverine said to the beautiful women.

"We ain't going to no party" said the tallest one.

"So why ya'll looking so good like ya'll going somewhere?"

"This how we dress all the time" the tall one responded again feeling Wolverine's style.

"Everybody calls me Wolverine" Wolverine said extending his hand.

"Well it's nice to me you Wolverine my name is Candy" she said shaking his hand.

J-Murder parked right behind the Range Rover that stood in front of him. "Damn whoever owns this Range Rover got his weight up" J-Murder said.

"There go that nigga Wolverine go right there "Rico said pointing at him. Rico and J-Murder both pulled out their Uzis and walked up to the glass and shot it out.

Wolverine stored Candy's number in his cell phone when out of the blue he heard gunfire and shattering glass. The shots ripped through Wolverine's flunky and the two women like a hot knife through butter. When Wolverine finally realized what was going on he quickly grabbed Candy and threw her in front of him as a shield. As the bullets hit Candy's body Wolverine managed to pull out his Desert Eagle and fired back BOOM BOOM BOOM BOOM Wolverine then felt two shots hit his bullet proof vest and another hit his arm. The impact from the shot caused Wolverine to hit the floor. They quickly hopped in the hooptie and fled the scene.

When Wolverine heard the gunfire come to an end he quickly pushed Candy's bloody body from off the top of him and staggered to his feet and looked at the four bodies on the floor. "Damn I gotta get the fuck up outta here" Wolverine said holding his bloody arm. When Wolverine finally made it outside he could hear the sirens already. He opened the door to his Range tossed the gun in the passenger seat hopped in the driver seat and put the petal to the metal.

* * *

CHAPTER FIFTEEN

Wolverine sat in his crib getting head from his shorty and smoking a blunt. "These niggas think they can do that to me?" He asked himself taking another drag from his blunt, "I got something for that ass" Wolverine said pulling out his cell phone and dialed a number. Rocks answered the phone on the second ring. "Yo what's good son?"

"Yo what's good my youth"

"Chilling busting this nigga Sticks ass in Madden why what's up?"

"This nigga Rico dumped on me tonight" Wolverine said. "Word to my mother B but you know them niggas can't see me I took one in the arm. Outta 50 shots them punk ass niggas only hit me in the arm one time, them niggas ain't gangsta. I'm gonna show them niggas how to do this"

"Nah fuck that me and Sticks gonna tighten that nigga right up for you"

"Good looking make sure ya'll get his ass cuz if ya'll don't then I'ma have to pay his Mom's a little visit" Wolverine said.

Married To Da Streets

***

Rico sat on the bench along with Buck eating some Chinese food waiting for J-Murder to show up. Trina had just bought a new house and the whole crew was supposed to go and congratulate her.

Meanwhile Rocks sat in the passenger side of the stolen Chevy while Sticks sat in the backseat. Rock's little flunky J.J was the driver. "Yo I know exactly where them niggas be at" Rocks said as him and Sticks loaded their Mac 10's.

Rico and Buck cracked a bottle of Moet still waiting for J-Murder to show up. "Damn B where the fuck this nigga at?" Rico stated plainly taking a swig from his bottle. "Yo I just called this nigga and he still ain't answering his jack (phone)". As the two men sat waiting for J-Murder it started pouring down raining. Rico and Buck ran and stood in front of the building to get out the rain. As Rico took another sip from the bottle he felt his cell phone vibrating. Rico looked at the caller ID and saw that it was Trina. "What's good baller?"

"You tell me is ya'll still coming?"

"We waiting for this nigga J-Murder that nigga was supposed to been here. Yo as soon as that nigga get here we over there"

"Rico I don't care if nobody shows up you better come and see my crib I worked so hard for. I don't give a fuck what time you come as long as you get here" Trina said.

"Say no more Ma I got you"

Thirty minutes had passed and J-Murder still hadn't showed up yet. "Yo something ain't right" Rico said to himself as he pulled out his cell phone, and called his crib. After 8 rings the answering machine picked up. "This bitch gonna fuck around and make me kill her" Rico said as he dialed Trigger's number. "Hello what up Trigg?, Yo where the fuck is this bitch at?"

"She wit that same cat from before wit the waves" Trigger replied.

When Rico heard that he was heart broken. "Where the fuck they at right now?"

"They at the BBQ's on seventy something street, you know which one I'm talking about right?"

"Yeah I know where they at but yo check this out I'm on my way over there, if they make moves before I get there hit me on the hip and let me know what's good" Rico said furiously. "Yo I gotta make moves B" Rico said giving Buck and the rest of the crew pounds.

"So what's up wit Trina's crib tonight?" Buck asked.

"Nah we probably gonna have to do that tomorrow" Rico said taking another swig from his bottle as he jogged to his Benz so he wouldn't get too wet.

Rico pulled off and hit an illegal U turn. "I'ma kill me a mufucka tonight" Rico said stopping at the red light and taking another swig from his bottle.

"Yo ain't that Rico's Benz right there? Sticks asked as they stood at the red light on the other side of the street. "Yo I can't tell the niggas tints are too dark and it's fucking raining too hard" Rocks said looking at the jet black Benz with the heavily tinted windows.

"Who the fuck is these clowns bumpgottenat new D Block shit" Rico said taking another swig from his bottle. "I wish them niggas would try to front" Rico said looking at his 9mm sitting in the passenger seat. "Them mufuckas lucky I got business to take care of" Rico said stepping on the gas.

"Nah at ain't him" Rocks said as the two cars passed each other. "Nigga you sure?" Asked Sticks. "Yeah son I just got a good look at the driver and that wasn't Rico".

"Aight yo J.J slow dis mufucka down, there them niggas go right there" Sticks said rolling down the windows. "Let's do dis" Rocks said also rolling down his window. When the Chevy got to the front of the building that Buck and the rest of the crew was standing in front of Rocks and Sticks let them have it RAT TAT TAT TAT. The rest of the bullets hit the crew and tore up the front of the building. Rocks and Sticks made sure they laid everybody down before the Chevy left the scene of the crime.

* * *

Rico made it to BBQ's just in time to catch J-Murder and Tiffany coming out of the restaurant. Both huddled up under an umbrella. Rico watched as J Murder opened the car door for Tiffany being a perfect gentleman. Rico just sat and watching feeling disgusted taking another swig from his bottle as he watched J-Murder pull off. Rico followed the Impala listening to the soft sounds of Mary J Blige. Mary always helped him stay calm. Rico followed J-Murder to the Days Inn and just watched as J-Murder and Tiffany jogged to the lobby of the hotel to get out the rain. "I can't believe dis nigga J gonna try to play me like this" Rico said taking another swig from his bottle. "I bring you to the top wit me and this is how you pay me back?" Rico said pulling his silencer out the glove compartment. "Everybody wanna be the fucking man CLICK CLACK" Rico said cocking his 9mm in one hand and his bottle of Moet in the other. Rico walked up to Triggers car and tap on the window with the toast. "Yo fams get up outta here cause I'm about to turn it up in this bitch" Rico said taking another swig from his bottle. "You sure you gonna be alright in there by ya self?" Trigger asked.

"Yeah I got this my boy"

"You should just wait until they come out?" Trigger suggested.

"Man fuck that I ain't got time for dat shit you just make sure you get up outta here" Rico barked at him.

"Aight Rico good luck, Oh yeah and before I go my Lil Man called me and said Wolverine came through and sprayed shit up a few minutes ago and he said Buck got killed and like six other niggas that was down with the team got merked too"

"Listen Trigger this shit is over take ya money and get the fuck up outta New York it was fun while it lasted" Rico said as he walked off. Rico walked in the lobby of the hotel dripping wet, clutching his 9mm.

Rico walked right up to the desk clerk and pointed the 9mm right at her head. " Yo I'm only gonna ask you this once, a woman wearing a red shirt just walked up in her wit a kind of stocky gentleman, what room are they in?"

The frightened woman stuttered "room # 311". "Good looking Ma" Rico said taking another swig from his bottle as he made his way to the staircase.

Rico stood in front of room # 311 and took another swig from his bottle before he shot the lock off the door and kicked it in. Rico walked in the room and saw J Murder and Tiffany both sitting on the bed reading a piece of paper that Tiffany held in her hands.

"Oh shit what's good my nigga?" J-Murder said walking up to Rico to give him a pound. Before J Murder got close enough to give him a pound Rico had already aimed the 9mm at his best friend and pulled the trigger, PST. Tiffany sat there in shock as she watched J-Murder's brain pop out the back of his skull.

"Rico what the fuck is wrong wit you!?" Tiffany screamed at the top of her lungs, "you fuckin crazy, what you wanna spend the rest of ya life in fucking jail?"

"Shut the fuck up" Rico said as he back slapped Tiffany with the heat (gun). "Bitch you wanna run around and fuck my best friend, what you thought I wouldn't find out" Rico asked aiming 9mm at Tiffany's head.

"Ain't nobody fucking nobody" Tiffany said crying like a newborn baby. "We was trying to throw ya stupid ass a surprise birthday party you jealous bastard!"

"Bitch what I look stupid to you?" Rico yelled.

"If you don't fucking believe me just go look on the dresser"

Rico picked up a piece of pink paper that read "Surprise Birthday Party For The One And Only Rico if you don't have a flyer you won't get in.

When Rico read the flyer he felt like a real sucker.

"What's wrong with you?" Tiffany asked holding the side of her face.

"Yo I gotta get up outta here" Rico said taking a swig from his bottle. "Yo grab J Murder's keys out his pocket and take his whip home.

"Nah I'm just gonna take a cab home" Tiffany said grabbing her things. When Rico made it back to the lobby he saw the clerk on the phone surrounded by 5 guys wearing hotel security uniforms.

"The fuck is ya'll niggaz looking at?" Rico said as he dumped on all 6 of them leaving blood everywhere. After Rico shot the desk clerk in the face he took another swig from his bottle and walked out the hotel never noticing the surveillance camera watching him the whole time.

Rico hopped in his Benz threw on his windshield wipers and headed straight for the liquor store where he purchased two more bottles of Moet. Rico hopped back in the Benz and popped one of the bottles open, and took a long swig. "What the fuck did I just do?" Rico asked taking the clip out of his 9mm. "Fuck that I ain't going back to jail, them fucking crackers gonna have to kill me" Rico said as he pulled off and headed to his stash crib. As Rico pulled off he never noticed Cali and his man Can't Get Rightfollowing him in a gold Maxima. "Yeah I got something for ya punk ass" Cali said as he continued to follow Rico.

CHAPTER SIXTEEN

Rico was on the highway when he felt his cell phone vibrating, he looked at the caller ID and saw that it was Kim. "Yo what's up?"

"Nothing I was just thinking about you baby, what you doing?"

"Yo I gotta get up outta here, this bitch Tiffany done got me in some shit"

"Tiffany?" Kim echoed. "I'ma bust her ass" Kim said getting real ghetto.

"I don't care what you do to her but that safe I got in ya crib the combination is 36, 9, 13. It's about $ 75,000 in there take that money and hold it. If I make it safe outta town I'll call you to join me but if I don't make it take the money and invest in something" Rico told her "Your gonna make it Rico stop thinking negative all the time"

"Listen I gotta go I'ma holla at you". Rico hung up his phone and turned the volume up and bobbed his head to Jim Jones's "Certified Gangsta" taking another swig from his bottle. Rico pulled up to his apartment in the Bronx that only he knew about and hopped out the whip. When he got inside the crib he filled two duffle bags to the top with crisp stacks of money. He then grabbed the .45 that laid on the counter and stuck it in the small of his back. When Rico made it back downstairs he placed the two duffle bags in the trunk and head to Trina's crib.

Det. Ford sat in the hotel looking at Rico acting like a madman on video tape. "I finally got the son of a bitch, there's no way your gonna beat this one. I got your dumb ass on tape" Det. Ford said rubbing his hands together. Within 15 minutes Det. Ford had the whole NYPD looking for Rico.

Rico pulled up to Trina's driveway and shut the car off. "Damn her crib looks better then mines" Rico said taking another swig from his bottle. Rico then pulled out his cell phone and called his crib, Tiffany picked up on the second ring. "Rico?"

"Check this out, I'm getting outta town, When I get situated I'm sending for Yasira aight?"

"What about me Rico?" Tiffany said.

"What about you?" Rico said coldly.

"So you just gonna dog me like that, after everything we been through?"

"Bitch you made me kill my best friend!"

"I didn't make you do anything, ya insecurity made you kill ya friend"

"Yo whatever, the combination to the safe is 13, 6, 21. I got like $ 120,000 in there take that shit and start you a new life aight?"

"Rico I don't want a new life, I can't live wit out you. If I can't live with you I don't want to live at all. Rico please don't do this to me, I love you and I'm the mother of ya beautiful daughter. I would do anything for you and you know it"

Rico hung up I. Her her face.

When Tiffany hung up her phone she heard somebody banging on the door like the fucking police. "Damn I don't even feel like talking to no police right now" Tiffany said as she walked to the door.

Kim stood on the other side of the door with her face greased, her hair pulled back in a ponytail and some sweatpants on. As soon as Tiffany opened the door Kim punched her in the mouth and pushed her back in the crib. The two beautiful women went crashing through the coffee table sending glass everywhere. "Bitch what you thought you was gonna try and put my man in jail and wasn't nothing gonna happen to you" Kim said as she punched Tiffany in the face again.

"Bitch get off of me" Tiffany said as she grabbed a hand full of Kim's ponytail and pushed her from over top her.

"Ya man, bitch Rico is my husband" Tiffany screamed as she lunged towards Kim and punched her in the face. The two both put their heads down and just started punching wildly on each other destroying everything worth value and tearing the house up until Det. Ford ran up in the crib along with 10 other officers wearing riot gear and broke up the catfight.

"Get on the fucking floor" Det. Ford said violently throwing Kim and Tiffany on the floor and threw the handcuffs on both of them. Det. Ford and the other officers then searched the crib from top to bottom. searching for Rico.

* * * * * *

Trina answered the door wearing a short green nightgown with the matching lime green slippers. " I see you finally made it, shit I was about to go to sleep" Trina said stepping to the side to let Rico in.

"Congratulations this house is what it is" Rico said handing Trina a bottle of Moet.

"You hungry, I got some fry chicken in the kitchen you want some?"

"Nah I'm good"

"Aight come let me give you a tour of the crib" Trina said excitedly. After Trina finished giving Rico a tour of the house the two sat down on the bed in the master bedroom and started shooting the breeze.

"You know I had to shut shit down right?" Rico said.

"What you talking about?" Trina asked while taking a sip from her glass.

"Yo after I leave here I'm going outta town and I ain't ever coming back"

"Why what happened?" Trina asked.

"The game is over, Buck and the rest of the crew is dead"

"Dead! What happened?" Trina asked in shock.

"Wolverine came through and sprayed shit up and took out the whole crew. And on top of that I ain't fucking wit Tiffany no more and I had to kill J-Murder tonight" he told her. "It's a long story Ma, I'm just stressed out yo"

"Don't worry everything is gonna be fine" Trina said massaging Rico's shoulders.

"Everything happens for a reason Rico and I'm quite sure there is a reason for all of this"

"I hope so Ma but chesaifyis out, I want you to take some of that money you made and open up a Beauty Parlor or something cause this hustling shit is a rap" Rico said dropping knowledge.

I'll do whatever you want me to" Trina said.

"I want you to take care of ya self while I'm gone you hear me?"Rico asked looking Trina in her eyes. "No more of that fast cash shit you got enough money to just fall back, settle down and just live the good life"

"Okay Rico whatever you want me to do I'll do you don't have to ask me twice"

"Aight I'm about to get up outta here, you take care of yourself you hear me?" Rico said as he stood up to leave.

"So I guess dats it huh?" Trina asked as her eyes got watery.

"Yeah I guess this is it" Rico said as he grabbed Trina and threw her into a bear hug. "Yo I'ma miss you Ma no matter what you was always there for me but yo I gotta get up outta here but don't worry I'ma keep in touch wit you cause you know..." Before Rico could finish Trina kissed him on the lips.

"Whoa" I don't know if we should..."

"Shh" Trina whispered as she threw her tongue in Rico's mouth. Trina snatched Rico's shirt off and backed him into the wall. As Trina continued to kiss Rico she dug in his waistband and pulled out his 9mm and tossed it on the floor she then grabbed the .45 from the small of his back and tossed it on the floor also. "I been waiting so long for this" Trina whispered in Rico's ear at the same time licking it. Trina unstrapped Rico's bullet proof vest and removed it as she explored Rico's upper body with her hands. Rico ripped Trina's nightgown off and looked at Trina's fatty sitting in the lime green thong. Rico then quickly knocked everything off the top of the dresser on to the floor and sat her on top of the dresser. Rico snatched Trina's thong off and started eating her pussy. Rico kissed, nibbled, and licked Trina's clit until she came back to back. Trina then hopped off the dresser and pushed Rico backwards until he fell on the bed. She took his pants off and was surprised to see how big his dick was "Uhm dats what I'm talking about" Trina said as she threw that big dick in her mouth, Trina sucked Rico's dick like it was a popsicle. Rico just sat back and watched Trina's juicy lips slide on and off his dick. Trina was sucking his dick so good that her mouth sounded like a pussy. "Oh shit Ma I'm about to cum" Rico said as he grabbed a hand full of Trina's hair and exploded in her mouth. Trina continued to suck Rico's dick until it was rock hard again. Rico then turned Trina over and just looked at her body for a second. Trina laid spread out on the bed on all four's waiting for Rico to pipe her down. Trina's pussy was throbbing from anticipation. With Trina bent over on all four's her ass looked even fatter and from where Rico was standing he could see that Trina's pussy was soaking wet. Trina let out a soft moan as she felt Rico slide inside her walls.

"Oh shit, I love you" she moaned as she felt Rico's dick in her stomach. Rico spreaded both of Trina's ass cheeks apart as he slid in and out of her. "This what you wanted right?" Rico asked as he slapped Trina's ass. "Ahww yes baby fuck me Rico" Trina moaned as she came all over Rico's dick. "Oh shit I'm about to cum again" Trina moaned as she threw the ass back at Rico. Rico grabbed a hand full of Trina's hair with one hand and grabbed her waist with the other hand as he erupted inside of her.

"Yo I gotta get up outta here" Rico said as he got dressed. "Listen I'ma keep in touch wit you and once I get settled you can come down and visit"

"Rico why can't I just go wit you?" Trina asked looking Rico in his eyes. "I've loved you since we were kids and ain't no other bitch gonna ever hold you down like I do" Trina said as her eyes started to water. "Rico we were meant to be together" Trina said as she kissed his lips.

Rico thought about it for a second, and for some reason he just couldnt tell her no. "Yo hurry up and go pack ya shit"

"Oh thank you so much" Trina said as she jumped in Rico's arms and flooded him with kisses. Forty five minutes later Trina was ready to go.

"You sure you got everything?" Rico asked.

"Yeah I'm straight"

Rico carried Trina's bags to the Benz and threw them in the trunk.

"Shit I must really love you cause I'm giving up This nice ass house I just bought to be on the run wit you" Trina said as she pushed Rico's back up against the driver's side door and tongued him down.

***

"Yo there them mufuckas go right there" Cali said as he cocked his AK47 and stood up through the sunroof.

When Rico heard screeching tires he immediately pulled out his 9mm and let off a few rounds until he heard the sounds of an AK47 spitting. Rico quickly jumped in front of Trina and covered her as he felt multiple bullets rip through his bullet proof vest. As Rico fell on top of Trina she quickly pulled the .45 from his waistband and let off five shots in the moving car's direction. One of the five shots hit "Can't Get Right" in the neck causing the car to spin out of control and run dead into a light pole. Trina turned Rico over and saw blood coming out of his mouth.

"Oh my God Rico get up" Trina screamed trying to lift Rico up.

"This shit is over Ma" Rico whispered. "Get the fuck up outta here, grab my car keys from outta my pocket and get up outta here everything you need is in the trunk. Take the keys and start all over fresh down south somewhere cause it ain't no more love in the city".

"Rico I can't just leave you here I love you" Trina cried.

"Listen Trina if you really love then you will take the keys and go. Yo I'm starting to get cold,

Trina never forgetIthat I always loved you and I always will and do me a favor"

"Anything" Trina responded.

"Tell my daughter that I love her" Rico said as he faded away.

"Nooooooo you can't die what am I gonna do wit out you?" Trina said crying over Rico's dead body. "I Love You Baby" Trina said as she kissed Rico on the cheek and took the keys out of his pocket. Trina hopped in the Benz and backed up outta her driveway as the sirens got louder and louder. Trina threw the Benz in drive and stepped on the gas all the way to her destination.

SIX YEARS LATER

Trina sat in South Carolina in her condo watching Rico Jr. play his PS3 (playstation). Trina always showed Rico Jr. pictures of his father and everywhere she went she wore Rico's chain that she took from him the night he got murdered. Trina was doing everything in her power to keep Rico Jr. from turning to the street life when he got older. Trina left all the drugs, murders, and partying in New York. She was now a mother and a Nurse's Aide. Before she went to bed every night she always looked at the picture of her, Rico and J-Murder that she had on her dresser. "I miss you guys so much" Trina said to herself as she stared at the picture. "If you had the chance to start life all over again would you do the same shit all over again?" Trina asked herself.... "You motherfuckin right"!!

***

Tiffany had moved on with her life. She was now married and about to give birth to another little girl. With the money Rico left her she opened up a Beauty Salon on 125th street. After Rico died she went and got a big tattoo on her arm that said "Rico". Rico would never be forgotten in Tiffany's or her daughter's hearts.

When Det. Ford found Rico laid out with his gun still in his hand he was the happiest man in the world. "One less nigger on the streets" he said to himself.

Cali lived after the car crash but was sent to the hospital, then arrested by Det. Ford. He is now serving 25 to life in Clinton Correctional Facility.

Kim has three kids now and is a secretary at a law firm. She also named her first son Rico.

Heather's mother Susan never got her shit together and is no where to be found. Heather is currently still living with Tiffany.

When Rico passed Wolverine took over his empire. He got every young brother in the hood walking around with a gun on them ready to pull the trigger at his command. Wolverine is currently going back and forth to court fighting an attempted murder charge he caught two years ago.

Sticks is currently in Mid State Correctional Facility doing a 3 to 6 year bid for drugs and an illegal fire arm (handgun).

THE END

NOW AVAILABLE ON
PAPERBACK

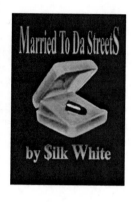

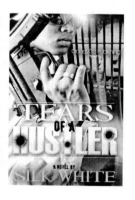

Silk White

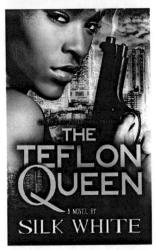

GOOD2GOFILMS PRESENT:

BLACK BARBIE THE MOVIE

STARRING SILK WHITE

ORDER NOW FROM

WWW.GOOD2GOFILMS.COM

$7.99

NO WAY OUT THE MOVIE

STARRING SILK WHITE

www.silkwhite.com

www.good2gopublishing.com

www.good2gofilms.com

CPSIA information can be obtained at www.ICGtesting.com
Printed in the USA
LVOW06s1337110815

449683LV00001B/270/P